THE ASSASSIN'S BETRAYAL

THE ASSASSINS
BOOK 2

MARK ALLEN

ROUGH
EDGES
PRESS

ALSO BY MARK ALLEN

THE ASSASSIN'S BETRAYAL

PROLOGUE

TWENTY YEARS AGO...

MALAKAI WAS ONLY sixteen years-old when he fired his first two bullets and he put them both into his father's medulla oblongata. Probably caught some cerebellum and hypothalamus too.

The bullets came from his father's gun, a 9mm Browning Hi-Power that he kept loaded in his nightstand drawer, right next to a black, battered, King James Version Bible and a dog-eared photograph of Malakai's long-gone mother. His father never bothered to lock up the gun because they never had any visitors and he didn't believe Malakai would ever dare touch the weapon.

He believed wrong. As he had about so many other things.

Malakai felt an alien sensation in his guts as he opened the drawer and took out the Browning. He tried not to think about it, but that was like asking a naked man in a blizzard to not think about the freezing cold.

Enough was enough. He could not—*would* not—live with this anymore. The horrible things churning around inside him were the final straw. His father was sick, twisted in the head with no hope of recovery. Sometimes when you're facing a mad dog that you once loved, you have no choice but to put it down. Malakai supposed you could call it mercy, but that would be a bullshit justification.

All he cared about was ending *his* pain, not his father's.

Still, whatever his reason for pulling the trigger, the end result would be the same.

His father was in the nondescript living room of their single-wide trailer, sprawled out in his favorite recliner, wearing holey-kneed jeans that hadn't seen a washing machine in at least a week and a grime-white tank top that was probably going on at least two weeks. Stereotypical white trash chic.

A goldfish tank sat on a rickety TV stand, full of slightly-greenish water but devoid of actual goldfish.

Those missing goldfish were the reason why his father had to die. Had those orange-scaled fish still been swimming stupidly around the glass bowl that made up their world, his father wouldn't be facing the end of his.

Malakai stepped into the room and raised the Hi-Power.

Some men face death with strength and dignity. They look the Reaper dead in the eyes and spit in his bony face. His father, like most bullies, was more of a piss-himself kind of guy. His eyes widened at the sight of the gun and he pleaded frantically. "Malakai...no... please, son... don't do this!"

He might as well have begged the earth to stop turning. Malakai fired two shots, one right after the other. *Bang-bang*. The rest of the trailer park would hear them, but he didn't care. As long as you didn't mess with their cold beer or welfare checks, they pretty much left you alone.

The first bullet snapped his father's head back, exposing the bottom of his jaw so that the second bullet burrowed under his chin and blew off the top of his skull. Gobs of brain tissue splattered the wall behind him like fistfuls of oatmeal thrown by an angry baby, and a spray of blood spattered the empty fish tank.

Malakai lowered the gun as smoke curled from the barrel, twisting up toward the ceiling like dragon's breath. He was right-handed, partly from nature, partly because the pinkie of his left hand was missing, gnawed down to a pink stump. It happened a long time ago, but some things you just can't forget. Or forgive. Just one more reason among many why his dad needed to die.

And yet, as he stared at his father's bullet-broken corpse, Malakai wept. The tears burned and stung, symbolic of his inner pain. He knew that his father, in his own dangerous, sadistic, fucked up way, had just been trying to help him. God knew it couldn't have been easy raising a young boy on his own after his wife pulled a Houdini and disappeared with that hot-stud Filipino yoga instructor.

Still, Malakai did not regret pulling the trigger. Good intentions did not excuse his father's actions. Some people just deserve to die and the world is better off without them and if anything his father had believed was true, then he was in a better place now.

As was Malakai.

He suddenly dropped the gun, doubled over

clutching his stomach, and threw up with a violent gagging noise. He felt them coming up, felt them in his mouth for a brief, horrifying moment, and then the four goldfish lay at his feet in a puddle of vomit, tails flipping weakly, no doubt as traumatized by having been swallowed as he had been by having to swallow them.

Malakai heaved a few more times, then spat to get the taste out of his mouth before he bent over and retrieved the Browning Hi-Power. "Fucking fish," he muttered as he raised the gun with a trembling hand and emptied the clip into them, blowing them apart in tiny bursts of guts and scales. No tears for them, that was for sure. In his world, the only good fish was a dead fish. From minnow to shark, he hated them all.

When the gun was empty, slide locked back on an empty chamber, he looked at his dead father. He felt like he should say something, anything. Sure, his dad deserved to die, make no mistake, but he also deserved some final words. Someone else would no doubt give a proper eulogy when they buried him, but for now Malakai reached deep down inside and found some words that seemed appropriate.

"Rest in peace, Dad, or rot in hell. Whatever God sees fit."

There was nothing more to say.

He thought about burning the trailer to the ground with his father's body in it, but decided that would be overkill. Instead, he packed his bags and hitchhiked his way down the east coast to southern Florida.

He never went back to his hometown. Never had a reason to. He had killed his own father. It would not be the last time he put a bullet in someone's brain, but it was the last time he did it for free.

CHAPTER 1

PRESENT DAY...

MALAKAI DIDN'T KNOW exactly how old the church was—well over a hundred, would be his guess—nor did he know why it was abandoned. He just knew he enjoyed the peace, tranquility, and solace he found sitting in the dilapidated pew in the dark of the Florida night, embraced by shadows. And God knew his life needed all the solace he could find. Sometimes he found it in a bottle; other times he found it in this dusty old church where ghosts and angels and perhaps even demons dwelled. The only illumination came from the moonlight slivering through the broken stained glass windows.

A large crucifix hung on the wall behind the cobwebbed pulpit, an exquisitely rendered and chillingly lifelike Christ figure stretched out in redemptive agony. Nothing unusual there; similar crucifixes could be found in ten thousand churches across the globe.

What was unusual about this crucifix was that someone had glued plastic toy guns onto each nail-pierced hand. Every time he came here, Malakai wondered what possessed someone to do that.

He was ready to go back to work. He'd taken a leave of absence to assist his former partner, Gabriel Asher, with tracking down Larissa, Gabe's girlfriend, and smuggling her across the border into Mexico. He had called in favors from some of his contacts to hook both Asher and Larissa up with new identities designed to give them a fresh chance at a life together, away from the shadow-world of blood and bullets.

Not that he had told the Company any of that, since they were the primary reason Asher and Larissa were on the run. They had sent a covert kill-team— Black Talon—to deep-six their former operative, but Asher decimated them. As a result, the Company issued a standing shoot-on-sight protocol for Asher.

But Malakai didn't give a damn about that. Asher wasn't just an ex-partner, he was a friend, and that meant more to Malakai than some misguided kill order. Besides, as far as he was concerned, the Company was being stupid and shortsighted about the situation. Asher was the best bullet-slinger in the business. They should have been trying to woo him back into the fold, not take him down.

Malakai mentally shrugged. *What the hell do I know? I'm just a hired gun, paid to put bullets in bad guys.*

Next to Malakai sat his handler, an enigmatic, middle-aged ex-priest with close-cropped, salt-and-pepper hair. Malakai knew him only as Father Thomas and although he still wore his clerical collar, his work no longer had anything to do with the Church.

His mouth pretty much proved that. "Why the fuck do we have to meet out here in this shithole? Everything we need to do can be done by computer. Establish a secure satellite link, run some encryption software, and bingo, no need to drag our unhappy asses out here in the middle of a goddamn swamp."

"My ass is happy," said Malakai. "And it's southern Florida, Tom. Everywhere is in the middle of a swamp."

"Smartass."

"So now my ass is happy *and* smart?"

"You still haven't answered my question."

"Maybe I'm old school," Malakai said. "Or maybe I'm just lonely and like the company."

"Buy a blow up doll." Father Thomas studied the modified crucifix. "Why do you think Jesus has guns?"

How the hell should I know? But instead of saying that, Malakai shrugged and put forth a theory. "Maybe somebody was trying to recreate God in their own image. Maybe somebody who lives by the gun thought it would be cool if God packed a couple of gats. Artistic expression and all that." He paused for a moment, then added, "Or maybe somebody was just bored."

"God and gats, huh?" Father Thomas managed to seem both annoyed and amused. "Sounds like Old Testament shit, all fury and vengeance and punishment. These are New Testament times. Now God is all about love and mercy and compassion. You should try it sometime, Quartet."

Father Thomas had nicknamed him Quartet years ago because of Malakai's penchant for using four bullets to kill a target. Not the coolest moniker, but he figured it was better than being called Can't Hit Shit or something like that.

"I know as much about mercy and compassion as a nun knows about the Kama Sutra," he said. "I know how to put a bullet in a target's head, that's about it. And let's face it, you and I both know I'm already damned anyway."

"We're all damned," Father Thomas muttered. "But what makes you say that?"

"I kill people for a living. Pretty sure that's not the best way to gain God's good graces."

"Take it from me, the grace of God is overrated." Father Thomas waved a hand dismissively. "Besides, you can kill people and still be forgiven. Except yourself. You can't kill yourself. Suicide is a one-way ticket to Brimstone Boulevard in Sulfur City. Do not pass go, do not collect two hundred, just take a fast train to Hell and start sucking Beelzebub's ball sack."

"I'll keep that in mind, but no matter how you spin it, I'm pretty sure I'm fucked." From anyone else, the statement would have sounded like self-pity; from Malakai, it simply sounded matter of factual.

Father Thomas started to say something else, but Malakai shot him a look letting him know this particular topic of conversation was over. The ex-priest knew Malakai's relationship with faith and spirituality was twisted and complicated, but his knowledge barely scratched the surface; he had no idea just how deep Malakai's scars ran when it came to such things. And Malakai had no intention of telling him.

Father Thomas handed him a folder and switched topics. "Here's your next assignment." He smirked and added, "Hopefully you can squeeze it into your busy schedule between all the beautiful women you're juggling."

"Don't be a jerk, Tom."

"Sorry," said Father Thomas, though he didn't sound sorry at all. "But it boggles my mind that you don't bother with women. Do your palm and your dick have matching friction burns?"

Malakai resisted the urge to whip out his FNX-45 Tactical pistol and plant a hollow-point between the ex-priest's eyes. The Company frowned on their freelance operatives going all bullet-happy on their handlers. So instead of putting another proverbial notch on his gun, he simply said, "I'm not discussing my love life with you."

"You mean your *lack* of a love life," Father Thomas needled. "AKA, lack of pussy."

"Love and sex aren't the same thing."

"Yeah, well, you aren't getting either one."

Malakai ignored him, opened the folder, and examined a photograph of a plump, doughy-faced man wearing a Stetson big enough to hold a keg of beer. "Give me the rundown."

Father Thomas buckled down to business. "Robert Olander. A Texas born and bred oil tycoon, in case the stupid hat didn't give it away. Three days ago we received word from our man inside the Syndicate that Olander is planning on getting into bed with them."

"What does the Syndicate want from an oil baron?"

"It's a back door plan," Father Thomas explained. "They don't really want Olander, they want his wife. You see, Robert Olander is married to Senator Paula Olander who happens to be head of the Senate Intelligence Committee, so of course she has access to all sorts of juicy secrets and the Syndicate wants to get their hooks into her. Obviously this cannot be allowed to happen."

"Who's your guy on the inside?" asked Malakai.

"Does it matter?"

"Just wondering how reliable your information is."

"You don't know the guy, but you've probably heard of him. Jack Cavanaugh."

"I've heard the name. Supposed to be one of the best undercover operatives in the game."

"He's not *supposed* to be one of the best undercover operatives in the game," Father Thomas said, "he *is* one of the best undercover operatives in the game. Which means this intel is gospel. If Cavanaugh says it's going down, then it's going down. Olander is coming to town tomorrow for some face-time with some Syndicate lackeys. We want you to intercept him."

"Meet, greet, and then six feet deep."

"That about sums it up, yeah."

"Give me the vitals."

"Olander's plane lands in Miami at 3:34 tomorrow afternoon. Two Syndicate bodyguards will escort him to the Crystal Tower Hotel. He's staying in the top-floor penthouse, so you'll have to get your hands on an access card. He should be settled in his suite by 5:30 and we expect him to stay there until at least 7:00."

"What makes you think he'll stay put?" Malakai asked.

"The Syndicate is providing him with a hooker and his meeting with them is scheduled for 7:30 in the hotel's nightclub. He'll have entertainment in his room and an appointment to keep, so there's no reason for him to leave."

"What about the hooker?"

"A Syndicate whore. Consider her collateral damage."

Malakai didn't kill innocents. Just like his friend Asher, he followed a creed, and while he didn't have a fancy, poetic name for it like The Assassin's Prayer, what it boiled down to was that he only targeted people that deserved it.

"What if I don't want to waste the bullet?"

Father Thomas gave him a piercing stare. "You going soft on me, son? I want hard cocks working for me, not limp dicks."

"Just asking a question."

"Waste the bitch or don't. Your call. That answer your question?"

Malakai nodded. "Anything else or are we done here?"

Father Thomas shifted in his seat as if uncomfortable with whatever he had to say next. "Actually, yeah, there is something else. The money handlers want me to talk to you about lowering your fee. You're charging thirty percent more than our other freelance contractors."

"You want top talent, you have to pay top dollar. Somehow I seriously doubt I'm breaking the bank." Now it was Malakai's turn to deliver a hard-eyed stare. "Don't play me for a sucker, Tom. My dad taught me that nobody can make you their bitch unless you let them."

"You're actually going to listen to advice from your dad?" Father Thomas sounded like that was the stupidest thing he had ever heard. "The man used to strip you butt-naked and beat your ass bloody with a big black Bible. No offense, Quartet, but your dad was a messed up son of a bitch who was a few cards short of a full deck, if you don't mind me saying so."

Malakai felt something cold and bitter trying to uncoil inside him. He honed a razor edge onto his words as he replied, "Actually, I do mind. Don't disrespect my father."

"Seriously? Don't disrespect your father?" The ex-priest blinked at him in disbelief. "You put two bullets in his head, for God's sake."

"Yeah." Malakai looked up at the crucifix again, wondered if there were answers to questions that his soul had not yet found a way to put into words. "But just because I killed him doesn't mean I didn't love him." He paused for a moment, hoping that Father Thomas couldn't see moonlight piercing the broken windows and betraying his moistened eyes with a revealing gleam. A blink, then another, and the glint of tears was gone. "So do us both a favor and shut your fucking mouth about my father."

Father Thomas held up his hands in the universal symbol of surrender. If he caught the glistening in Malakai's eyes, he decided not to comment. Probably knew he would be throat-punched if he did. "All right, okay, relax," he said, then sighed. "You need a shrink, man, you really do. You've got some issues." He paused, then said, "Just so we're clear, that's a 'no' on the rate reduction?"

"Damn straight it's a no," Malakai said. "I'm not some skid row junkie with a Saturday Night Special jonesing for my next fix and willing to pop a cap in someone's ass in order to get it. I'm a professional and therefore I make professional wages. Deal with it."

"We'll deal with it," said Father Thomas. "Just as long as you deal with Olander." He stood up, stretched his arms languorously as if he had just awakened from a nap, and then stepped out into the aisle. He paused there for a moment, looking up at the pistol-packing Christ impaled on the cross. He shook his head the way someone does when they just don't understand something. "Guns on Jesus. That's just messed up."

"Well, they did call Him a Peacemaker."

Father Thomas groaned. "Oh, that's so lame." He shook his head again. "You're a very strange individual, you know that?"

"I didn't put the guns there."

"Maybe not, but I wouldn't put it past you."

Father Thomas turned and left, his footsteps echoing in the emptiness of the deserted sanctuary as he walked down the aisle. Malakai heard the rusted hinges of the front door creak in protest as they opened, then repeat the noise as they closed. But still he remained in the pew, alone, save for the ghosts that haunted this place, the angels that stood guard, and his own personal demons that still rattled their cages from time to time. God help him if they ever got out.

He leaned forward, reached behind him, and pulled his FN FNX-45 Tactical semi-automatic pistol from a small-of-the-back holster, concealed beneath the shirt he wore untucked in the Florida heat. As he sat back in the pew, he ejected the magazine and then racked the slide, popping out the round in the chamber. It glinted in the shadows, moonlight sparking off the brass, until Malakai reached out his hand and caught it.

This church had once been a sanctuary for sinners, and so it was again tonight. Malakai suffered no delusions; of all the sinners that had sat in these pews, he was probably the worst of them all. He was a killer. Not for love or revenge or some other emotional justification, but for money. The root of all evil. Sure, everyone he put down deserved their bullets, but somehow he doubted God would care when reckoning day came.

Malakai squeezed the bullet in his hand, felt the cool metal against his palm, rolled it between his fingers. He did it without thinking, muscle memory, an automatic ritual that kicked in during times of reflection. Some people fondled a rosary; Malakai played with bullets.

He held the cartridge and gazed up at the cross. He had once had faith in the latter, but now the bullet had become his religion. Some people prayed a thousand prayers in their lifetime; he had fired a thousand bullets. He had been raised by his father to love the Lord, but now he served only the god of the gun. Somewhere along the way, he had lost his way.

Just call me the prodigal assassin.

He raised the .45 in the gloom of the sanctuary, locking the sights on the head of the crucified Christ. His father would have beaten him to a quivering pulp for such sacrilege. But his father was dead.

How about you, huh? Malakai asked silently as he looked into the eyes of the man nailed to the cross. *Do you want to punish me? Or maybe you already are. Maybe that's what this life is all about—punishment.*

Malakai shook his head as if to shake away the gloomy thoughts. He needed to lighten up. He was such a grim bastard sometimes. He lowered the gun, put the round back in the magazine, and then slammed the clip into the FNX. By this time tomorrow, that bullet would be buried in a man's body and the next time Malakai came to this church, there would be another sin on a soul.

He told himself that he didn't give a damn.

Part of him even believed it.

CHAPTER 2

THE HOT AND humid Miami heat was downright sultry the following evening, but the ocean breeze kissed away enough of the edge to make it tolerable. Well, tolerable if you dressed in shorts and a T-Shirt like a normal Floridian. Malakai, on the other hand, was sweating to death beneath the light jacket he wore in order to conceal the FNX-45. Rivulets ran down his body as heat waves shimmered off the sidewalk. Right about now he would have sold his soul to the devil for some air conditioning.

As he walked, he kept his steps erratic and unsure, his dark brown eyes—so dark, in fact, that most people thought they were black—hidden behind mirrored sunglasses. A white cane swept the pavement in front of him, forcing pedestrians to dodge around him. All part of his masquerade, his plan to infiltrate the penthouse suite of the Crystal Tower Hotel and put a bullet—or four—into Robert Olander.

The Crystal Tower Hotel rose twenty stories into the air and towered over its beachfront acreage. It was an octagonal structure that appeared to be constructed out of mirrors, every single angle and plane a reflective surface designed to catch the rays of the south Florida sun and send crystalline flashes sparking everywhere. It was a haven for the rich, the expensive price tag of a reservation more than ample enough to ensure only the wealthy relaxed, rested, and rutted on the sheets. The whole vibe and *feng shui* of the place made it perfectly clear that this was no pauper's paradise.

As Malakai approached the hotel, the stump of his missing left pinkie finger began to throb. It always did right before a hit. He had no idea why it happened—the missing digit had no association to his work—but it did every time, regular as clockwork. He suspected it had something to do with the adrenaline spike making his blood pump hotter and faster, but that was just a wild guess. Besides, he had long ago learned how to control the adrenalin rush associated with being a gunslinger. Whatever the reason, the missing pinkie throbbed, almost like a biological alarm alerting him that the moment of action had arrived.

Three steps led up to the hotel's entrance, each one so wide that it looked you could have thrown some hoops up on each side and played full-court basketball. Malakai successfully negotiated two of the steps, but pretended to catch his foot and trip on the third. He stumbled forward, all part of the act. Maybe not Oscar caliber, but good enough.

A doorman sprinted forward and grabbed his arm to keep him from taking a tumble. "Here, sir, let me help you." His tone brewed with the bow-and-scrape servitude the obnoxiously wealthy expect from the invisible staff that wait on them.

Malakai allowed himself to be steadied, twisting his body enough to ensure the helpful doorman didn't see the sound-suppressed .45 riding in a cross-draw position on his left hip, concealed beneath the light jacket. He seriously doubted the doorman's friendly demeanor would stay in place if he glimpsed a gun. "Thanks," Malakai said, making his voice rueful. "I'm still getting the hang of this whole blindness thing."

"You are more than welcome, sir. Enjoy your stay at the Crystal Tower."

Malakai nodded and moved past the doorman, faking a grateful smile as he surreptitiously slipped the access card he had lifted from the unsuspecting Samaritan into his pocket. His fingers knew how to do more than just pull a trigger.

Inside the hotel, Malakai continued to feign blindness as he maneuvered his way past the gigantic fountain dominating the floor of the lobby and headed for the elevators directly ahead, sweeping his cane in front of him. People politely moved out of his way as he approached. Behind his mirrored shades, he saw a tall, elegant woman visually stripping his 5'10", sleekly muscled frame as he passed and heard her say, "For a blind guy, he's kind of cute." As if all blind people were generally ugly.

Malakai rolled his eyes at her crassness and kept moving. There weren't enough bullets for all the stupid people in the world.

At the elevators, he pretended to fumble along the wall looking for the buttons. He found the "Up" button, pressed it, and waited. Somewhere above him, muffled in the shaft, he heard the sound of gears in motion as the car descended to ground level. Normally he wouldn't use an elevator on an assignment because you could be too easily trapped in one. But a blind man wouldn't take the stairs, so he needed to ride the lift in order to maintain his façade.

The car arrived, the doors opened, and he stepped inside. The patron saint of assassins must have been in a good mood, because nobody joined him. The doors slid shut and he pressed the button for the penthouse. A digital screen chirped at him and displayed the message ACCESS CODE REQUIRED. He swiped the pilfered card through the attached reader and within two seconds the screen message changed to ACCESS GRANTED. The car immediately began to ascend. The easy part was over. Now the real work was about to begin.

The ride up didn't take long, but it gave Malakai enough time to perform a last minute double-check on the .45. He pulled the slide back halfway to confirm there was a bullet seated in the chamber and gave the suppressor a good, hard twist to make sure it was screwed on tight. This was a hotel full of people. The last thing he needed was for anyone to hear a gunshot. This was not the south side of St. Petersburg where a shot might be ignored or mistaken for a car backfiring; the elite millionaires loafing around the Crystal Tower would instantly go into freak-out mode if they heard a gun go bang.

The car began to slow down and he holstered the FNX, letting his jacket fall back in place over the pistol. He gripped the white cane and got ready to play blind man once again. The throbbing in the stump of his missing finger intensified. It was almost game time.

The car halted, the doors hissed open, and he exited

into a hallway so lushly carpeted it was like stepping on a cloud.

He walked straight ahead, sweeping with his cane until he tapped the opposite wall, just like a blind man would do. At the same time, he used his peripheral vision to identify two bodyguards standing at the end of the short hallway that stretched to his right. They were braced on either side of the penthouse door. He would have to go through them to get to Olander.

Not a problem.

Malakai hesitatingly turned toward them, tapping with his cane, and then began his approach, moving the cane back and forth in front of him like a beachcomber using a metal detector to search for coins buried in the sand.

As Malakai drew near, Bodyguard #1, a hulking linebacker type with a shaved head and a gold hoop in his left ear, slipped his hand inside his sport coat where he obviously had a gun stashed. "I don't know how you got up here, boy," the brute growled, "but I do know that you need to drag your blind ass right back down."

Malakai kept coming forward, cane arcing in front of him. He was ten feet away and closing the gap. Any bodyguards worth their salt would have pulled out their guns by now, but not these two. Either they were under orders to play nice while they were inside the resort or they were just idiots. Maybe both.

"I'm terribly sorry, sir," Malakai said, "but I'm having trouble finding my room. Is this the second floor?"

Five feet and closing.

Bodyguard #2 was an absolute monster with a neatly-trimmed Fu Manchu mustache. He reached for

Malakai and it was obvious he did not plan on being gentle, blind man or not. No respect for the handicapped. "All right, dipshit," he snapped. "Time for you to go bye-bye."

"You know," Malakai said, "I was just thinking the same thing about you."

He raised the white cane with his left hand and triggered a mechanism in the handle that activated a hidden spring launcher. The small blade concealed in the end of the cane shot out like a mini-missile and speared Bodyguard #2 right in the eye, punching through the orbital socket to bite into the brain.

Bodyguard #1 barely had time to register his partner's abrupt death. His eyes went wide as he realized this blind man was actually a lethal threat. He started to yank out his gun.

A little too late and much too slow.

Malakai drew his .45 with the snake-strike speed that comes from endless hours of practice. He fired a shot through the suppressor into the man's throat at nearly point-blank range. The gun made a soft *phytt!* sound while the target's Adam's apple made a slightly louder popping sound as the bullet blew it apart like a sledgehammered walnut before exiting the back of his neck. Both bodyguards hit the ground at the same time, their lifeless faces bouncing off the carpet as their bodies twitched in synchronized death dances.

Malakai paused long enough to lean his white cane against the wall and pocket his mirrored shades—he would need to resume his disguise in order to effect his escape, but inside the penthouse the props would be unnecessary—then stepped over the pair of bloody corpses. Since guards had been posted outside, he suspected the door would not be locked, and he was right.

He shoved open the door and rushed into the penthouse with the FNX raised and ready, hunting for his primary target.

Given the man's girth, he was hard to miss.

Robert Olander sat on the sofa wearing nothing but a Stetson, a smile, and rolls of sweaty flesh while his hands mauled the beautiful, professionally moaning blonde as she bounced on his lap like a pogo stick. She was giving it her all and Olander looked like he was just seconds away from falling in love. But she let out a terrified yelp as the door flew open and Malakai invaded the suite.

Olander threw her aside like a rag doll and tried to stand up, but froze when he saw the .45 pointed at him. "Don't move," Malakai said. "Just pretend your ass is metal and that couch is a magnet, got it?"

Olander settled back on the sofa, looking extremely unhappy. Malakai couldn't blame him. A few moments ago he had been getting screwed, but now he was royally fucked. Still, he managed to rustle up some blister. "Do you have any idea who I am, son?" he asked with a Texas twang.

"Yeah," Malakai said. "A fat man with a hard-on. Now shut the hell up." He turned to the hooker, curled up in a frightened ball on the corner of the couch, doing her best to cover up the parts that men liked to look at the most. The modesty seemed kind of strange coming from a woman who got paid to spread her legs. Sometimes Malakai thought he would never understand people. "Get dressed," he told her.

As the girl scrambled off the couch and began

pulling on her clothes, Olander glared daggers at him. "You're deader than a castrated bull's cock, you know that, right? Not only am I married to one of the most powerful Senators in the country, but I have friends that will do things to you that you can't even imagine."

"Maybe," Malakai said. "But you won't be around to see it, because you're gonna be shaking hands with the devil in about thirty seconds."

"You won't be far behind me," Olander retorted.

"Threats from a dead man don't mean much."

"That's not a threat, it's a promise."

"Then it means even less."

Malakai turned his attention back to the whore. She slipped on her high heels and stood there, nervously awaiting his next command. She looked absolutely miserable, as if trying to figure out how she had ended up here, screwing for money and facing the wrong end of a .45.

"Turn around," he said.

Her lower lip quivered and tears sprang into her eyes, too brilliantly blue to be anything but cosmetic contact lenses. "Please don't kill me. I'll do anything you want. Just please, don't—"

"What I want you to do," Malakai interrupted, "is turn around."

She started to cry. "I don't want to die."

"You're not going to die. Not right now anyway. Now turn around."

She clearly thought he was lying. But, lower lip clenched between her perfect white teeth, she obeyed. She moved slowly and Malakai didn't blame her; she believed she was about to receive an executioner's bullet. Not exactly the kind of thing to put a spring in your step.

But he had no intention of killing her. She might be a whore, but that didn't merit a hollow-point to the head. Instead, he slammed the butt of his pistol into the back of her skull. She fell to the floor in an unconscious heap. Not the most graceful collapse he had ever witnessed; she hit the carpet in a loose-limbed pile and her short skirt slid up over one of the best asses Malakai had ever seen. No doubt that derriere fetched at least $800 a night, but he had neither the time nor inclination to stare. He had to deal with Olander.

Fear-sweat mottled the oil tycoon's face but he didn't cower and beg like so many others Malakai had seen. "What do you want with me, huh?" His voice was tough, especially for someone riding the wrong end of a .45.

But all the false bravado in the world wouldn't save him. Malakai had spent a lot of years in the killing game. Never once had he failed to carry out a hit and he didn't plan on starting today.

"You got into bed with the Syndicate," he said to Olander, "and that decision significantly shortened your life expectancy." He raised the FNX. "So are you ready or do you need a moment?" His finger took up the trigger slack.

Olander went out defiant. "Take your best shot."

"How about four of them?" Malakai didn't smile when he said it. He took no particular joy in an execution. It was just a job, nothing more.

He fired four times in less than two seconds, all lethal speed and efficiency. The suppressor quieted the shots but could not quiet the sound of the bullets impacting on flesh and bone. They made wet crunching noises as they tore open his trachea, punched into his chest, and shattered his skull. Olander twitched and jerked in a spastic corpse-dance before finally slumping lifelessly on the blood-soaked couch.

Malakai didn't hang around to admire his handiwork. He'd seen enough bullet-blasted bodies to haunt his dreams for years should the ghosts of his victims ever turn vengeful. He holstered the .45, retrieved his casings, and stepped back out into the hall.

He dragged both corpses inside the penthouse and pulled the spring-blade from Bodyguard #2's eye. It dripped with all sorts of nasty gunk so he wiped it clean on the man's shirt. Rude, sure, but it wasn't like the guy cared. He locked the door behind him, hung out the "Do Not Disturb" sign, donned his mirrored shades, retrieved his white cane, and exited the vicinity.

He was enjoying his first beer before anyone realized Senator Paula Olander had become a widow.

CHAPTER 3

JOE'S BAR & Grill might not have boasted the fanciest name on the block, but it was situated off the beaten path, away from the hustle and bustle and—most importantly—the tourists of Miami's main boulevards. Just one of the reasons Malakai liked it here.

Another reason was because it was one of the few joints in the city that served Red Dog, his beer of choice when he wanted to knock back a couple of cold ones. He freely admitted that other brews tasted better, but something about the beer's underdog—no pun intended—status appealed to him. Didn't make a whole lot of sense, but that could be said of any number of things in his life.

Joe's also featured an old-fashioned, honest to God jukebox that only played '80s hair metal, his favorite musical genre. No Beyoncé or Taylor Swift or Blake Shelton...just Mötley Crüe, Poison, and Bon Jovi before they started playing sucky music for soccer moms. Joe, the owner/bartender, had nearly spit his beer out the first time Malakai told him that his favorite song was "You Give Love a Bad Name" because of the opening lyric: "Shot through the heart and you're to blame." A little hitman humor.

The bar was very dim, even murkier than most bars, as if to hide the sins of those who came here to drink. Calling it a hole in the wall would be insulting, but calling it one step above a hole in the wall wouldn't be too far from the truth. The place really wasn't much to look at. Just a long bar down the right side of the room, a few tables scattered here and there, and the aforementioned jukebox shoved into the corner. Fancy was not a word in Joe's vocabulary and his drinking establishment reflected that. And not-fancy was exactly the way Malakai liked it.

He walked in and paused for a moment to scan his surroundings, keen eyes probing every shadow. An automatic act to him, as subconscious as breathing. He would have an easier time stopping the blood from pumping through his veins than he would ceasing to check for threats every time he entered a room.

Satisfied no immediate danger lurked in the vicinity, he proceeded to his usual seat at the end of the bar. And that was exactly how he thought of it: *his* seat. He had been coming to Joe's for more years than he could remember and never once had he seen anyone else park their backside on this particular seat. It was like the stool had become a pariah simply because he touched it.

Joe was an elderly black man so skinny he was just an ounce or two away from being described as skeletal. He wore a black shirt with a bright red bow tie, both of which worked in tandem to complement his grizzled gray hair.

He handed Malakai an ice-cold bottle of Red Dog as he sat down on his stool. "Evening, Malakai," he greeted. "Hey, did you know if you turn the Red Dog logo upside down it looks like Batman performing cunnilingus?"

He used the same line every night. All part of their ritual and apparently for Joe, the joke never got old. Malakai smiled on cue, just like always. "Yeah, Joe, I've heard that." He took a pull from the bottle then raised it in salute to his favorite bartender. "Thanks. That hits the spot."

"Don't mention it."

"Just pay for it, right?"

"Now you got the idea. How was work?"

"Work was murder," Malakai deadpanned.

Joe groaned and shook his head. Malakai had never revealed what he did for a living, but over the years Joe had pieced together the general truth, if not the specifics. But they had an unspoken agreement to never talk about it. Confession might be good for the soul but it had a nasty habit of straining friendships.

"Well, it could always be worse," Joe said. "You could be standing here every night slingin' brewskies to sorry-ass jokers like you."

"You're a real charmer, Joe. Always know just what to say to make a guy feel good about himself." Malakai glanced around the room as the jukebox began playing an '80s power ballad from some long-forgotten second-tier band. He noticed an attractive redhead sitting alone at one of the tables. She looked out of place. Joe's was not the kind of gin joint pretty single women frequented. She caught his eye and offered a smile. Malakai had to admit that it was a very nice smile.

Joe, all-seeing god of the bar, rarely missed anything and he didn't miss this. He nudged Malakai's arm. "What are you waiting for?" he said. "Go on over, try your luck, see if you can make that smile on her face last all night."

Malakai shook his head. "I don't have time for that crap."

Joe arched an eyebrow in disbelief. "No time for love?"

"No time and no need."

"That's not healthy, man."

The woman apparently realized Malakai was not going to return her smile, so she dropped her own and turned away. But not before both he and Joe caught the disappointment in her eyes.

"See that?" Joe chided. "You broke her heart."

Malakai shrugged. "She'll get over it."

"Maybe, maybe not. You don't know that. It's not always that easy. For example, have you ever gotten over your ickyphobia or however the hell you say it?"

"Ichthyophobia," Malakai corrected with a scowl. "And why do you have to go there?"

"Because it's the weirdest thing I've ever heard," said Joe. "I mean, seriously, fear of fish? What, all the real phobias were taken so you had to come up with a bullshit one?"

"It's not bullshit," Malakai said. "Fucking fish scare the hell out of me."

Joe glanced at the stub where Malakai's pinkie used to be. "Because of what happened to your finger."

"Yeah, because of what happened to my finger." Bad memories tried to claw their way to the forefront of Malakai's mind. He drove them back by chugging his beer until the bottle was empty, then slid off his stool. "Sorry to cut this lovely chat short, but time for me to hit the road."

"Hot date?"

"Bite me, Joe."

The bartender chuckled. "And here I thought you said you didn't have time for love." He took the empty Red Dog bottle and set it in the sink before wiping down the counter. When Malakai reached for his wallet, Joe waved him off. "On the house tonight," he said. "Go home and get some rest. Big day tomorrow."

Malakai ignored him and tossed a fiver on the bar. Another one of their rituals. Every night Joe told him not to pay and every night he paid anyway. "What's so special about tomorrow?" he asked.

"It's your birthday."

Malakai groaned and rolled his eyes. "I have got to stop telling you personal shit."

Joe scooped up the money with a grin, teeth flashing white in the ebony of his face. "Hey, if you're a good boy and don't cause no trouble, maybe I'll buy you a present. Any requests?"

"Just as long as it's not you jumping out of a cake wearing nothing but that bow tie."

"Of course not. I'll be wearing my socks too."

"There's a mental image I could have done without," Malakai said as he headed for the door.

Joe feigned hurt. "Never mind then. I'll just buy you an aquarium instead."

As he exited the bar, Malakai called back over his shoulder, "Not funny, Joe."

The bartender chuckled and waved goodbye. As he rinsed out the empty Red Dog bottle, he glanced over to where the spurned redhead had been sitting. The chair was empty. Apparently she had moved on to greener pastures.

Joe shook his head and muttered, "Oh, Malakai, sometimes you are one stupid son of a bitch."

CHAPTER 4

LIGHT from the bloated silver moon shined down on the luxurious beachfront mansion and gleamed on the razored edges of the glass shards embedded in the top of the ten foot-high brick wall that encircled the entire estate. As protection went, the setup was pretty basic. Standard Security Enhancements 101.

But brick walls and broken glass were hardly the mansion's singular means of defense. No expense had been spared to protect the man who lived inside these walls.

The entrance gate was solid enough to stop a tank and guarded by two sentries toting KRISS Vector SMGs, cutting edge submachine guns uniquely designed to nearly eliminate recoil and muzzle rise which in turn increased accuracy. Difficult weaponry to obtain and the fact that the entire twelve-man security team owned one offered proof of the wealth and influence of the man the guns protected.

More Vector-armed sentries patrolled the grounds with a pair of attack-trained Dobermans. These dogs were not trained to bite an arm or a leg to incapacitate an intruder, they were taught to go straight for the throat. Not that it was likely to happen, but God help any Jehovah's Witnesses that made it to the front door. Hard to tell people about the Kingdom with a couple of Dobermans chowing down on your windpipe.

More passive defenses were also in place. True to the overcautious—some might even say paranoid—nature of the man who owned the estate, surveillance cameras were strategically mounted everywhere with overlapping fields of view to ensure not an inch of ground remained in a blind spot. Motion sensors lined the driveway that formed a circle in front of the mansion, an ornate fountain burbling at its nucleus. Hidden lighting made the water glow crystal-blue in the night. The mansion itself resembled a fortress, an eclectic combination of medieval architecture and post-modern industrial chic in which stone, steel, and concrete vied for dominance.

This was the residence of the man known only as Tanaka, head of the Syndicate's east coast operations. From New York to Florida, anyone associated with the Syndicate rarely made a move without his knowledge and those that did paid a terrible price. The marionette master of a criminal empire, he pulled the strings from behind the walls of his fortified estate.

Deep inside the mansion was a large circular room with a massive pool and stone pillars towering up to the cathedral ceiling that was painted with scenes of samurais and dragons and various other Japanese folklore.

Tanaka stood at the edge of the pool and stared down into the water. He was a middle-aged Japanese man with facial features that would be considered strikingly handsome in his homeland were it not for the harsh edges. He was dressed in an impeccable Brioni business suit. The large yellow rubber gloves he wore were in stark contrast to the calm, controlled poise he and his tailored clothes projected. They also sent a message that even though he ruled this criminal kingdom, he was not afraid to get his hands dirty.

A large plastic bucket perched on the edge of the pool next to his feet, which were encased in Barker Black dress shoes. He bent over, reached into the bucket, and pulled out a human arm, severed at the elbow. Blood still dripped from the limb, indicating the freshness of the amputation. As nonchalantly as feeding food flakes to a goldfish, he tossed the appendage into the pool where it slowly sank toward the bottom. The water's resistance made the fingers wiggle as if waving goodbye. Tanaka found the imagery quite fitting.

A sudden, silent blur of motion and then the water roiled violently as a fifteen-foot tiger shark snatched the arm in its jaws and swam away. Its head thrashed from side to side as its serrated teeth sheared through the dead flesh and crunched into its grisly meal.

Tanaka smiled as three more sharks glided toward him like silent torpedoes. His pets knew it was feeding time. He reached back into the bucket and this time pulled out a human leg, severed mid-thigh. The gnarled knot of protruding bone showed the ragged marks where the chainsaw teeth had cut through.

Tanaka remembered how the victim had begged him to put a bullet in his head first, but Tanaka was not a man prone to mercy. Living dismemberment seemed more appropriate for his enemies than a quick death. He flipped the leg into the pool and watched the water explode into a furious frenzy of foam and fins. And teeth. Lots and lots of sharp teeth.

Tanaka showed his own cosmetically-whitened teeth in a smile that was the epitome of serene. Without fail, witnessing the pure, primal savagery of his sharks brought him a sense of peace. Sometimes he wished he could dive naked into the pool and swim among them, feel their power up close and personal, pulsing against his skin.

The sound of footsteps echoing through the cavernous pool room pulled him from his reverie. He turned slightly and saw his assistant approaching. Yoshi was also Japanese, having accompanied his employer to the United States from Japan when Tanaka was honored with oversight of the Syndicate's east coast operations. Tanaka found Yoshi's subservient demeanor extremely satisfying. He did not need to be told he was one of the most powerful men in the country, but constantly being reassured of that fact by Yoshi's ceaseless bowing and scraping—more servant than assistant, truth be told—certainly didn't hurt. All men have egos and Tanaka knew he was no exception. The trick was to keep that ego on a tight leash and not let it out to play too often.

Yoshi stopped a few feet away and bowed at the waist. "Tanaka-san, we have just received unfortunate news."

"How unfortunate?"

"It is my deep regret to inform you that Robert Olander was assassinated a few hours ago."

"Did we not supply him with protection?"

"Two of our best, sir. They were killed as well."

Tanaka sniffed derisively. "Then clearly they were

not our best." Even if the two bodyguards had survived the attack on Olander, Tanaka would have executed them for their failure to protect the client. He did not suffer fools or failures kindly, and clearly the two men had been both.

Inwardly, the news of the assassination filled Tanaka with seething anger. But he controlled it, as he controlled everything in his life. Showing no outward sign of being perturbed, he reached down and pulled a human heart out of the bucket. He tossed it to the sharks as nonchalantly as an old man feeding bread crumbs to pigeons in the park.

As one of the aquatic predators swooped in and gulped down the still-warm hunk of cardiac muscle, Tanaka asked, "Do we have any leads on the assassin?"

"Actually, yes," Yoshi replied. "We believe the shooter was a freelancer by the name of Malakai. Mr. Olander was shot once in the throat, twice in the chest, and once in the head. That's Malakai's signature."

"Not that it matters, but what about the whore?"

"He let her live."

Tanaka arched his neatly-trimmed eyebrows. "Interesting. It would seem our assassin has a soft spot."

"So it appears," Yoshi agreed.

"Softness is weakness," Tanaka said as he shook blood off his rubber gloves. The red droplets spackled the surface of the water and increased the sharks' agitation. "Do they know about the photos?"

"We're not sure," Yoshi replied.

"What about the nephew? Do they know about him yet?"

"Unclear at this point," said Yoshi. "We simply do not know how much intelligence Cavanaugh forwarded to his handler before we found out who he was working for."

Tanaka reached down and pulled a severed head from the bucket. He held it aloft and stared into the rolled-back eyes. "Dead men tell no tales," he murmured. "Isn't that right, Mr. Cavanaugh?" He lowered the decapitated head and looked at Yoshi. "I want this Malakai found. We are the Syndicate and a message must be sent: nobody crosses us and lives. Nobody. Track him down and have one of our Miami people pay him a visit."

"It has already been set in motion, Tanaka-san."

"Excellent. Thank you, Yoshi."

Yoshi bowed and scurried off as Tanaka tossed the head to the sharks and watched them rip it apart, chunks of bone and brains crunching between their gnashing teeth. As always, his face remained calm. He viewed the violent destruction of a human body with the same serenity as someone watching a hummingbird sip nectar from a flower.

He glanced down into the bucket. All that was left inside was Jack Cavanaugh's blood, inches deep at the bottom. Cavanaugh was the second undercover agent the Company had tried to insert into the Syndicate. The second time that agent had died a horrible death.

Tanaka pulled off the rubber gloves and dropped them into the bucket. *That's right,* he thought. *Nobody messes with the Syndicate.*

CHAPTER 5

WHEN MALAKAI LEFT JOE'S, he took a meandering route home to his apartment, thinking the drive would help clear his head. He rolled the windows down in his 2019 Corvette Stingray and went for a cruise, letting the night air rush into the interior. In some cities, the spiffy sports car would have been too high profile for someone in his line of work, but in sun-soaked Miami, hot cars were a dime a dozen and nobody paid a Corvette a second glance. Had he wanted attention, he would have needed something seriously more exotic. Maybe a Lamborghini Aventador or something like that. But it wasn't attention he craved, it was peace.

But tonight the drive failed to put him at ease. Instead, it merely gave his inner demons the time and opportunity to wake up and claw open his psychological doors. By the time he got home, he had relived far too much of the hell his father had put him through. He drowned the demons in Jack Daniels with a couple of Red Dog chasers and crawled into bed.

But not even bad memories and booze-induced

sleep could dull his survival instincts. Some primal alarm system pulled him out of his slumber just in time to see a knife stabbing toward his face.

He reacted to the threat instantly, jerking his head to the side. The knife buried itself in the pillow. You couldn't have fit a feather between his cheek and the steel blade. He immediately stiff-fingered his attacker in the throat, driving him back.

Only it wasn't a "him", it was a "her".

The redhead from the bar.

What the hell?

Malakai reached for his .45 on the nightstand, fully intending to blast a bullet between her eyes. But she was far quicker than he anticipated. She surged forward before he could grab the gun, whipping the knife viciously back and forth like an '80's slasher jacked up on speedballs. He rolled out of bed naked and onto the floor to avoid getting carved up. As he hit the carpet, he lashed out with his foot and caught the woman's ankles, bringing her down to his level.

He rolled toward her, swinging an elbow into her chin along the way. As her head snapped back, he completed the roll and found himself on top of her, straddling her waist. An awkward position since he wasn't wearing any clothes. But if he hadn't wanted to bang her at the bar, he sure didn't want to bang her now that she had tried to shove a knife through his sinuses.

She might have been on her back—not her first time, he was betting—but she wasn't done fighting. She drove the knife toward him with her right hand. He easily deflected the blow, but he missed her left hand snaking in to play dirty. She grabbed a handful of balls and twisted with the viciousness of a woman scorned.

"You should have just fucked me," she hissed. "At least then you would have died happy."

A snappy comeback would have been appropriate, but all Malakai could do was grunt in pain through clenched teeth. He knew he shouldn't relinquish his superior position, but testicular agony overrode his desire for tactical advantage. He rolled away and climbed to his feet. He was slower than usual due to the pain and nausea slamming through his system. The woman was much faster, executing a perfect reverse backflip to spring to her feet like some kind of ninja-cat. She instantly lunged toward him yet again, blade sweeping in from the side, seeking to punch between his ribs and poke a nasty hole in his heart.

All he wanted to do was clutch his brutalized nuts, but instead he blocked the blow with his left forearm while simultaneously using his right fist to deliver a short, sharp rabbit-punch to the redhead's sternum. Right between the breasts he had turned down earlier this evening. The sharp, cracking blow meant it was her turn to grunt in pain.

She brought her knee up fast and hard, hoping to pulverize his already punished balls. Malakai turned his body sideways, toward her knife-hand, and took her knee-strike in the thigh instead. The thick meat and muscle absorbed the blow, but he knew there would still be a bruise there come morning. Assuming he survived until morning.

As he rotated away from her rising knee, Malakai chopped the edge of his palm across the wrist of her knife-hand, sending fire blazing through all sorts of nerve endings. The knife slipped from her suddenly-spasming fingers. Still in motion, Malakai caught the weapon in mid-air and drove it deep into her stomach. He gave the blade a quick twist to maximize internal damage, then released the handle as the woman stumbled backward, blood spilling from the wound.

Malakai grabbed his .45 off the nightstand, all locked and loaded with a round in the chamber. His throbbing scrotum cried out for vengeance, begging him to just blow the bitch away. But he wanted some answers first.

He pointed the gun at the redhead. "Who the hell are you?"

She leaned against the wall, both hands wrapped around the handle of the knife buried in her abdomen. When she looked at him, he saw nothing in her eyes but resignation, a calm acceptance that she had been bested. She didn't say anything.

"I asked you a question," Malakai rasped. "Who are you? Who sent you?"

The woman dropped to her knees. She pulled out the blade slowly, with nothing more than a slight wince.

Had he not been pissed at her, Malakai would have been impressed with the redhead's level of pain tolerance. But right now the only thing she could do to impress him was start giving him some answers.

With the gun still aimed at her face, he said, "You got a speech impediment? Start talking or we'll see if you can catch bullets with your teeth."

The woman closed her eyes. She breathed deeply for a second or two. Then, without warning, she jammed the knife under her jaw. Through her slightly parted lips, Malakai glimpsed the blade penetrating up into her mouth. Her movements trance-like, she dragged the knife sideways, cutting her throat open from ear to ear in a blood-gushing mess. Eyes still closed, she swayed and gurgled for a few moments, then toppled forward, dead before her suicidal face smacked the carpet.

Malakai blinked a couple of times and then lowered his gun. "Well, there's something you don't see every day." It felt like the understatement of the year.

He didn't stand around gawking. He had a corpse to deal with and the fact that the corpse—before becoming a corpse—had attacked him in his own apartment meant this location was compromised. Time to exit the vicinity.

He picked up his cell phone and dialed Father Thomas' number. Knowing his handler, he was probably in the middle of a *menage a trois* with a big-breasted blonde and a perky-assed brunette, but Malakai didn't care.

The ex-priest didn't answer the first time, so Malakai tried again. This time Father Thomas answered on the fourth ring. His voice couldn't have sounded grumpier if someone had rubbed his scrotum with sandpaper. "This better be an emergency," he growled. "I'm in bed and I've got a blonde with huge tits on one side of me and a brunette with the most perfect ass you've ever seen on the other."

Malakai didn't have time to gloat about his prophecy skills. He said, "Of course it's an emergency. I don't call you for social chats."

"So why did you call me?"

Malakai distinctly heard slurping sounds on the other end of the line. He shook his head and said, "The Syndicate paid me a visit. Things got messy. I need a cleaner."

"Things are about to get messy here in a few seconds," the ex-priest said with a groan.

"Stay focused, Tom."

"Yeah, yeah, I got it. The Syndicate. How did they find you?"

"Good question. I'll work on that later. Right now I just need someone to take out the trash."

"Hold on a sec," Father Thomas said. Malakai heard a long, slow groan, followed by, "Thanks, baby, you're the best. There's some mouthwash in the bathroom. Help yourself." Then he returned his attention to Malakai. "Okay, I'm back."

"Feel better?"

"Much. One day they'll name a vacuum cleaner after that girl."

"And they say chivalry is dead."

"Anyway," Father Thomas said, "I know a guy. Goes by the name of Mr. X. Used to work for the mob before we recruited him. I'll get him over there ASAP and he'll have the place cleaner than the pope's prick in no time."

"How long?"

"How long is the pope's prick?"

Malakai sighed. "No, jackass, how long before this Mr. X shows up?"

"An hour. Maybe two. Not sure how long it will take him to sanitize the situation. Want me to set you up at one of the safe houses?"

"Negative. I'll make my own arrangements."

"Copy that," said Father Thomas. "Meet me at the church tomorrow night. We have a loose end that needs tying up."

"I'll check my schedule."

"Just be there."

Malakai hung up, packed a large duffel bag with enough clothes and weapons to tide him over for the foreseeable future, and then left the apartment. Until he figured out how he had been burned—and by whom —he wouldn't be coming back.

He hopped in the Corvette and took Biscayne Boulevard into one of the seedier sections of Miami, where the motels charged by the hour, names were never asked for, and a few extra greenbacks greasing the clerk's palm ensured faces were never remembered.

When the clerk handed him his room key, Malakai noticed a rust-colored splotch on the plastic fob. "Is that a bloodstain?"

The clerk grunted. "Listen, pal, if you're worried about stains, you've come to the wrong place."

The guy had a point. Malakai nodded, pocketed the key, retrieved his bag from the car, and went to his room. It was pretty much exactly what you expect from a flophouse. Peeling, smoke-stained wallpaper. Thread-bare carpet. Cheap furniture. Cigarette burns on the bedspread. The kind of place you came to get your rocks off quick and cheap, not to get a good night's sleep.

As if to prove the point, a headboard in the adjacent room began banging off the wall and a whore's fake cries of passion came through loud and clear. She even threw in some compliments. Malakai wondered if her trick actually believed his was the biggest she had ever seen.

Yeah, it was a sleazeball's paradise, but he didn't have much of a choice. Somebody had burned him and when you have a rat lurking in your midst, sometimes you have to find a hole to hide in until you can bait the trap.

He locked the door behind him and fastened the security chain even though it looked about as strong as a dry-rotted rubber band. He then grabbed a straight-backed chair from the rickety desk and wedged it under the doorknob. A classic security improvisation. It wouldn't prevent anyone from gaining access, but it would slow them down long enough for Malakai to be ready with a few hollow-point surprises. Any knock-knocks would be followed by some bang-bangs.

He set the .45 on the nightstand, kicked off his shoes, and then stretched out on the bed fully clothed. The slamming headboard in the next room picked up speed and the whore's not-quite-Oscar-worthy moans tripled in volume, but he folded the pillow around his ears and managed to fall asleep in less than three minutes.

————

Further up the coast, far removed from the seediness of Miami's underbelly, Tanaka was not sleeping, nor was he thinking about Malakai. They had dispatched an assassin to kill an assassin and he fully expected a report any moment that the man responsible for executing Robert Olander was dead. They had used the fire-haired beauty to lure men to their deaths before and he saw no reason she would fail this time.

So instead of thinking about his Malakai problem, Tanaka found himself thinking about his daughter. They were not pleasant thoughts.

He sat in his large, spacious office behind a marble-topped desk so massive you could park a battleship on it. On the wall to his left loomed a bank of surveillance monitors that allowed him to view the mansion and surrounding grounds from any angle. A smart-screen flush-mounted in the desk allowed him to control the cameras with a simple touch of his fingers. Adjacent to the screen, up in the right hand corner of the desk, a *wakizashi* sword rested in a wooden cradle. The handle of the sword was wrapped in black cord filigreed with crimson threads.

Next to the *wakizashi* was a photograph in a minimalist metal and glass frame. As he picked up the picture and looked at it, his eyes softened. A rare event, permissible only because there was no one there to witness his moment of weakness. In the photo, he was a much younger man and in his arms he held his infant daughter. It had been a different time and he had been a different person. Perhaps even a better person, if he was being completely self-honest.

For just a couple of heartbeats, his eyes moistened, but then the office door swung open as Yoshi entered and Tanaka blinked away whatever tears might have come.

Yoshi stood in front of the desk and bowed, ever subservient. "Tanaka-san, I am sorry to disturb you."

Tanaka waved away the apology. His mind still roamed elsewhere, traveling the shadowed paths of nostalgia. "Yoshi," he said thoughtfully, "do you think my daughter will ever stop hating me?"

Yoshi squirmed like a salted snail, clearly uncomfortable with the question. Which was no surprise; he was accustomed to business questions, not family affairs. "Sir, it is not my place to say. I hope so. I know how much her forgiveness would mean to you."

Tanaka gently traced his fingers across the glass covering the picture. "Truth be told, her hatred hurts me more than I sometimes care to admit." He sighed, then put the photograph back in its usual place next to the sword. He had wasted enough time indulging in a past he could no longer change. Time to pull himself together. He leaned forward, hands clasped on the desk in front of him, and said, "Now, what is it you wished to speak with me about?"

Yoshi looked grateful to be back on familiar territory. "We just received word that the hit on Malakai was a failure."

Tanaka remained outwardly stoic—his face could have been carved from granite—but inwardly this unwelcome news displeased him. He was not a person prone to thinking in vulgar terms—he believed such to be a sign of low breeding—but this Malakai was becoming a pain in the ass. And the Syndicate did not suffer fools, failures, or pain in the asses lightly.

He touched a button on his smart-screen, then rose from his chair and walked to the back of the office. Large panels slid open, revealing a floor-to-ceiling bulletproof window that looked out over the beach. The security wall that surrounded the estate blocked the view of the ocean, but the moon-spackled sand still offered a soothing sight. Tanaka folded his hands behind his back and gazed out into the night. Without turning around, he asked, "The woman we sent to take care of this job?"

"In accordance with Syndicate law, upon her failure, she took her life."

Tanaka nodded. Outsiders might not understand, but it was as it should be. "Then she died with honor. See to it that her family is compensated for their loss." He turned away from the window for a moment and spoke over his shoulder. "And, Yoshi?"

"Yes, Tanaka-san?"

"Our plans for Senator Olander can afford no further setbacks. I want this Malakai problem dealt with. Call the Twins."

Yoshi blanched slightly. "Sir, with all due respect, are you certain you wish to call in a wrecking ball when a scalpel might suffice?"

"What I am certain of," Tanaka replied, "is that I do not intend to underestimate this Malakai again. It is possible to kill a fly with a chopstick, but a shotgun ensures the job gets done. Make the call."

"Of course, sir." Yoshi pulled out his cell phone and dialed a number in Australia.

———

While it was nearing the witching hour in the United States, the sun shone bright and sunny in Sydney. A houseboat rocked gently on the postcard perfect waters of Sydney Harbour within excellent viewing position of the famous Sydney Harbour Bridge and Opera House, but the three houseboat occupants were not taking in the sight because they were inside taking care of business.

For two of the occupants—Jesus and Joseph Twin— that business was beating a man to pulp for no reason. Well, there was a reason, but they didn't know what it was. Nor did they care. They had been hired to beat the man to death and that's what they were doing, no questions asked.

The third occupant's business was being the victim of the beating.

A blindfold covered the victim's eyes and he was bound to a wooden chair, face just a punch or two away from looking more like raw hamburger than anything resembling a human visage. Whatever his sins were—if indeed they were sins at all; guilty or innocent, it didn't matter to the Twins—he was paying for them dearly.

Joseph Twin, a muscular blond who could have moonlighted as the poster boy for the Aryan Nation, worked the man over with a pair of brass knuckles, displaying the skill of a true professional. Feet braced wide to counter the rocking of the boat, he delivered a short, sharp, savage series of blows that whipped the doomed man's head to one side, then back the other way, flinging blood and sweat in both directions. The meaty thud of brass striking flesh almost drowned out the annoying cries of the ever-present seagulls wheeling around outside.

His brother, a huge, burly Hispanic named Jesus, leaned against the wall and watched with eyes colder than a dead snake set in a pockmarked face that was far too rough to be handsome. A thin mustache draped each side of his cruelly twisted lips. A Skorpion submachine gun was slung over his shoulder. Not his favorite SMG but it spat bullets and killed men and that was all Jesus really cared about.

He stared dispassionately—this was just a job, nothing more—as Joseph delivered a nose-breaking blow to the man in the chair. His nostrils flattened and splattered like a hammered strawberry.

Over the wet crackle of crunched cartilage, Jesus heard his cell phone activate, his ring tone set to the chorus of "Kick Ass" by Egypt Central. He found it funny, even if nobody else did.

He tapped the screen to accept the call and raised the phone to his ear. "Jesus Twin." His deep, gruff voice pronounced his name "Jee-zus", not the traditional Hispanic "Hay-zeuss". Nobody really knew why except Jesus himself. Wasn't like anyone was going to mistake him for their Lord and Savior.

On the other end of the line he heard a weak, slightly feminine voice that never ceased to annoy him, no matter how many times he heard it. Thankfully the little bastard didn't call him too often. "Mr. Twin, this is Yoshi. Mr. Tanaka asked me to contact you."

"Yeah?" Jesus grunted. "What do you want?"

"Is Joseph there with you?"

"Yeah. Now do me a favor, don't waste time with any stupid chit-chat, and just tell me what you want before I book a one-way trip to Japan and kill your mother for giving birth to a worthless piece of trash like you."

"Of course," Yoshi said with his usual ingrained deference. "My apologies."

Jesus shook his head in disgust. What a pathetic excuse for a human being. Threaten to murder his mother and he remained as polite as if you had just asked him to pass the salt. Some people were just born weak, and Jesus despised weakness.

On the other end of the line, Yoshi was still speaking. "Have you heard of an assassin named Malakai?"

Jesus' interest was immediately piqued. Maybe this phone call hadn't been a waste of time after all. "Yeah, we've heard of him. One of the best guns for hire in the business, probably second only to Gabriel Asher. Hell, they might be equals."

"Surely Malakai isn't better than the mighty Jesus and Joseph Twin."

The slight taunt in Yoshi's voice made Jesus want to choke him to death. "Nobody is better than us," he growled.

"Excellent," Yoshi replied, "because Mr. Tanaka would like to hire you to take out Malakai. He has become something of a thorn in our side. Can you handle the job?"

"Sure we can handle it," Jesus said, "but a job of that caliber will cost you double the usual rate."

"Double seems a bit steep."

"It is steep, but so is the risk. It's also non-negotiable. Take it or leave it."

Yoshi sighed. "Fine. How soon can you get to Miami?"

"As soon as we're finished here."

"And how long that will be? We need this Malakai matter resolved sooner rather than later."

"A rush job." Jesus shook his head and muttered, "I should charge you triple."

"I am not authorized—"

"Yeah, yeah, shut the hell up." He looked at Joseph, who was taking a break from beating the man. "How long before we're done here?"

Joseph tapped the bloodied brass knuckles together and shrugged. He never spoke. Not that he couldn't; he just chose not to. The silent partner in the relationship, the quiet yin to Jesus' bellowing yang. Any talking that he needed to do, he did it with a weapon or fists.

Jesus rolled his eyes. "Hold on a second," he said into the phone, then set it down on a small table next to him. He unslung the Skorpion, pointed it at the man in the chair, and pulled the trigger. The slugs hammered a bunch of ragged holes in the target's chest and the high-velocity impacts tipped the chair over backwards so the man's feet stuck straight up in the air. Were it not for the blood splattered everywhere, it would have been almost comical, like an autofire rendition of some slap-stick routine.

No, scratch the "almost" part. To Jesus, it actually *was* comical. After all, funny was in the eye of the beholder. With a smirk on his pock-scarred face, he picked up the phone and said to Yoshi, "We're done here. Be there in a day or two."

"Excellent," said Yoshi. "We will look forward to—"

Jesus hung up on the sniveling weasel. He had a dead body to dispose of, a boat to burn, and a plane to catch. As he went to work with a variety of sharp uten-sils, carving the corpse into chum for the sharks that lurked in the harbor, a wide smile creased his face. Not because of the grisly task at hand, but because of their new assignment. They were going to cross swords with Malakai. Jesus knew him only by reputation, but that reputation got the warrior blood pumping hot through his veins, the kind of thrill-rush he hadn't felt in a long time.

Jesus. Joseph. Malakai.

It was going to be one hell of a fight.

CHAPTER 6

WHEN FATHER THOMAS entered the old church, he saw no sign of Malakai. He was alone save for the haunted shadows in every corner and the demons that lived in his own heart.

He gazed around the sanctuary and muttered, "Damn it, Malakai, if punctuality were a sin, you'd be a saint." He had once told his top bullet-slinger that he would probably be late to his own funeral, to which Malakai had replied that he didn't plan on dying, so that wouldn't be an issue.

Father Thomas strolled down the aisle between the rows of dusty pews until he stood before the altar. He paused there for a moment, a thousand memories racing through his mind as they always did when he found himself in a holy place. But when one memory in particular clawed its way to the surface, he forced it back down into the dark depths where it belonged. He didn't want to think about that. Not here. Not now. Not ever.

He stared up at the crucifix and at that moment

would have sworn that the stone eyes of the crucified Christ stared back at him with the peculiar mix of care and condemnation that the Good Book so often attributed to God Almighty. Father Thomas had never really understood how the Lord could be so forgiving one moment and so ferocious the next. He secretly thought the Bible made God look bipolar.

As if to atone for his blasphemous thoughts, he immediately crossed himself. Even though he hadn't performed the act in a long time, he did it flawlessly, the motions ingrained in his muscle memory. It was the relapsed Catholic version of riding a bike.

"Bless me, Father, for I have sinned," he murmured, his voice barely loud enough to be heard above the song of insects in the swamp outside. "It's been a long damn time since my last confession."

God failed to answer...unless His answer was to have Malakai ghost out of the shadows, tuck a gun against Father Thomas' temple, and say, "So let's hear it, padre. Gotta warn you though, the penance could be pretty severe. Almost getting killed in my own bedroom has kind of left me in a bad mood."

Father Thomas did the smart thing—he held very, very still. Only his lips moved, just enough to demand, "Where the hell did you come from? And what the hell are you doing?"

"Trying to figure out if you burned me or not."

"Really?" Father Thomas sounded legitimately dumbfounded. "You seriously think I sold you out?"

"Somebody did," said Malakai. "Not too many people know where I live. If it wasn't you, then make me a believer."

"It wasn't me and you know it," Father Thomas

snapped. "You're a Company contractor and that means there are files on you, files that can be leaked, hacked, stolen."

"Thought those files were classified and buried deep."

"They are, but have you watched the news lately? Nothing is completely hack-proof. Listen, did somebody sell you out to the Syndicate? Damn right they did. But it could have been anyone associated with these black ops. The only thing I know for sure is that it wasn't me."

Malakai kept the FNX pressed tight to his handler's head, the muzzle dimpling the skin. "Then who was it?"

"The fucking Easter Bunny," Father Thomas growled. "How the hell should I know? But if you aim that gun somewhere that doesn't run the risk of me receiving a forty-five caliber lobotomy, I'll put out some feelers."

Malakai stared at him long and hard, then lowered the gun. The ex-priest probably deserved a bullet for a lot of bad shit, but the only thing Malakai cared about right now was who had burned him and he couldn't lay that betrayal at Tom's feet. But it needed to be laid somewhere. "I want a name," he said.

Father Thomas walked over to the front pew and sat down. Any other man would have sported a piss-stain on the front of his pants, but not him. Amateurs soiled themselves, not professionals. The ex-priest had spent far too long in the game to be rattled by facing the wrong end of a gun.

"Off the top of my head," he said, "I can tell you one

suspect that comes to mind, but I don't think you want to hear it."

"Just tell me."

"Your bartender."

Malakai holstered the FNX and sat down as well. "You're kidding, right? Joe doesn't know where I live."

"Doesn't need to know where you live to give you up," Father Thomas pointed out. "You go to his dive practically every night for that Red Dog swill you call beer and that glam-metal noise you call music. All he had to do was tell the Syndicate which bar they could find you at and they could've tailed you from there."

"That's quite the theory you've got there," said Malakai. "Got a motive to go with it?"

"Money—what else? Your boy can't be making too much money in that shithole, and the Syndicate is probably offering an obscene amount of cash for your head on a stick. Maybe your friend saw an opportunity."

"You're forgetting something."

"What's that?"

"He's my friend."

Father Thomas rolled his eyes. "Try acting like a professional instead of some ditzy bitch, will you?" He waved at the crucifix on the wall. "That guy hanging up there is a prime example of someone who got fucked over by a friend. One minute your buddy is giving you a little peck on the cheek, the next minute he's got a pocketful of blood money while you're getting the goddamned nails. When there's nothing but lint in your pockets, thirty pieces of silver can be one serious temptation."

"Nice speech," Malakai said. "Did you just call me a ditzy bitch?"

"That's what you got out of all that? Sometimes I really hate you."

"That's progress. You used to hate me all the time."

"Listen," said Father Thomas, "I'm not saying Joe's your Judas; just throwing it out there as a possibility. I'll do some digging, see what kind of worms I can turn up."

"Speaking of digging things up," Malakai said, "there's something I always wanted to ask you—what made you stop being a priest anyway?"

Father Thomas' jaw abruptly clenched as he stared at Malakai. Had he been able to see behind those haunted eyes, Malakai might have caught a glimpse of hell, the disturbing memories that tormented his handler's mind. A church sanctuary. Worship twisted into wounds. An unholy abomination. Sacred innocence defiled. A young boy weeping. Sickness and wickedness and tears and shame. And a man of God with broken vows.

But of course, Malakai could see none of this. All he could see was the haunted eyes and clenched jaw and extrapolate how horrible the memories must be that tortured the ex-priest's mind.

Father Thomas answered him through gritted teeth. "Something happened."

"Well, thanks for clearing that up," said Malakai. The ex-priest clearly had some issues to work out. But then, who didn't? Saints and sinners alike, everyone had their demons. The trick was learning how to live with them. "Want to talk about it?"

"God, no," Father Thomas replied quickly, as if the very thought of discussing the matter horrified him. "I'd rather cut my own dick off with a rusty butter knife."

"Makes me wish I had a rusty butter knife right

about now," Malakai said. "That might be interesting to watch."

Father Thomas snorted. "You just want to see my pecker."

"Unfortunately, I have seen it. It's next to the word 'diminutive' in the dictionary."

The ex-priest glared at him. "There's something wrong with you. You know that, right?"

"There's something wrong with all of us." Malakai shrugged. "Since you don't want to talk about what made you become a man of the gun instead of a man of the cloth, tell me about this loose end that requires my attention."

Father Thomas handed him a folder. "For the record, you're not the only one who's been burned. Somebody blew the cover on Cavanaugh. He wasn't as lucky as you. A box showed up at the office yesterday with a severed finger inside and a note that said 'For DNA purposes'."

"You run it?"

"No, I sent it to the taxidermist to have it stuffed. Thought it might make a nice paper-weight." Father Thomas scowled. "Of course we ran it and yeah, it's Cavanaugh. Poor bastard. They said it was cut off with a chainsaw. Those Syndicate sons of bitches are fucking savages." He shook his head in disgust. "Anyway, the last time Cavanaugh checked in, he fed us some intel about a guy named Jim Abbott with connections to Robert Olander. He's our loose end."

Malakai opened the folder and studied the photograph of a clean-cut man in his thirties with a close-cropped, military style haircut.

"Jim Abbott," Father Thomas recited. "Ex-Marine and, more importantly, Robert Olander's nephew. Turns out he is in possession of some extremely explicit and highly embarrassing photos of his aunt, the Texas senator. We're not exactly sure of the contents of the pictures at this point, but word is that a donkey, handcuffs, and about a dozen jars of Peter Pan peanut butter were involved."

"All the ingredients for the perfect Disney movie."

"With Robert Olander dead, thanks to you," Father Thomas continued, "the Syndicate can't sink its hooks into the senator that way, so they're going to their backup plan: good old-fashioned blackmail. Abbott has agreed to sell the photos to the Syndicate who can then use them as leverage to force the senator to play ball with them. Abbott's flying into Tampa two days from now to visit his brother in Saint Petersburg. While he's there, he's also meeting with the Syndicate to do the exchange."

"Why are they having an actual meeting?" Malakai asked. "Abbott could just email the pictures and the Syndicate could deposit the cash in his account electronically."

"The pictures are Polaroids," Father Thomas explained. "They were taken in the senator's younger days, before there were digital cameras."

"They could still be scanned and sent."

"Syndicate wants the originals. More leverage. We want you to intercept Abbott, take him out, and retrieve the photos."

"Another black bag dance, right?"

"You chose to play the game," Father Thomas said, "so don't bitch about the rules. You mess up, you're on your own, but if you find your ass in a sling, I'll do what I can."

"Words are cheap," said Malakai. "Right now, as far as I'm concerned, every word out of your mouth could just be smoke up my ass."

"Now why the hell would you say some shit like that to me?"

"Because there's a Judas out there, Tom. And since I have no desire to be nailed to a cross, your name is staying on my list of possibilities."

Father Thomas shook his head. "You're a faithless fuck, you know that? But whatever. Just be careful when you go after Abbott. He's an ex-Marine, not some helpless target. Remember that."

"The day I need you to tell me how to do my job is the day I hang up my guns."

"Boy, you're cranky tonight."

Malakai got up and headed for the door. "Almost getting killed in your own bedroom will do that to you."

Father Thomas remained seated in the pew, but called over his shoulder, "Malakai, I know he's your friend, but don't scratch Joe off your Judas list without at least having a conversation."

Malakai grimly replied, "Don't worry, I'm going to have a conversation."

CHAPTER 7

MALAKAI LEFT the church with a troubled mind and drove straight to the bar. The darkness of the night mirrored his thoughts. He rolled down the Corvette's windows to see if the influx of fresh air would improve his mood, but it just let in the humidity, which definitely did not improve his disposition.

He didn't want to believe Joe was capable of betraying him, but he knew Father Thomas was right—he couldn't rule out the possibility. This conversation was going to be about as much fun as getting a colonoscopy with a power auger.

There were more people than usual in the bar. Which meant there were about three. Def Leppard rocked the jukebox, singing about liking it hot, sticky-sweet, and covered in sugar.

As Malakai approached his favorite stool, Joe popped the cap off a Red Dog and set it on the bar. "There's the birthday boy. You're running a little late tonight," the bartender greeted. "Hey, did you know that if you turn the Red Dog logo upside down it looks like Batman performing cunnilingus?"

Malakai ignored both the beer and the ritualistic joke. "We need to talk," he said. It came out harsher than intended.

Joe arched an eyebrow at his friend's tone. "About anything in particular or are we just going to pick random subjects?"

"Not here. In the back."

Joe didn't move. "What about my customers?"

"They can wait," said Malakai. "This won't take long." *Especially if I have to put a bullet in you.*

"What if someone steals from the register while we're out back playing diddly-dicks?"

"I'll kill them when we're done."

Joe stared at him for several long seconds, probably trying to figure out exactly what the hell was going on, then shrugged. "Fine." He tweaked his bow tie. "Follow me."

Malakai followed Joe into the back storage room. Neatly stacked cases of beer towered everything, floor to ceiling, creating a warren that required a map to fully navigate. The place smelled like booze, but that was to be expected.

They didn't walk too deep into the maze before Joe turned and faced Malakai, his posture stiff. Not yet angry, but ready to be if necessary. "Okay," he said, "I'm all ears."

Malakai subscribed to the theory that if something was going to hurt, it was best to get it over with quick, so he didn't waste any time. "Listen, Joe, you know what I do for a living, right?"

Joe held up his hands, a look of alarm on his face.

"Whoa, whoa, whoa! Hold it right there. What the hell kind of conversation is this? Do I know what you do for a living? No, I don't."

"C'mon, Joe. That's bullshit and you know it."

"Do I have my suspicions? Can I put some of the pieces together? Sure, 'cause I ain't stupid. But my suspicions are just that—suspicions. I don't want them confirmed or denied. I don't want to know jack-all about what you do when you're not here." Joe lowered his hands to his side and gave Malakai a serious look. "You and I, we don't talk about that crap, man, because as far as I'm concerned, this bar is your sanctuary, your church, your holiest of holies. Your sins and secrets don't matter here and I don't want to know them."

"I appreciate that, but we still need to have a chat."

"Then do us both a favor and keep it vague."

"Fine." Malakai plunged into a conversation that no man ever wants to have with someone he considers a friend. "I've made enemies, Joe. Enemies who want me dead, enemies willing to pay a lot of money to whoever helps make me that way." He looked Joe straight in the eye. "You see where this is going or do I have to ask the hard question?"

Joe could not have looked more dumbfounded if Malakai had said he was dating a mermaid and rode dragons for a hobby. "You're asking me if I sold you out? Seriously?"

Malakai felt lower than snail slime, but he couldn't let emotions get in the way of answers. "Somebody did, and I don't have many friends." Actually, he didn't have *any* friends other than Asher and Joe. Not because he couldn't socialize, but because he didn't care to.

"Well, it wasn't me," Joe said, his voice emphatic

and wounded. "And if you ask me about it again, I'll take that gun you've got tucked under your jacket away from you and shove it so far up your ass you'll be shitting bullets for a month straight." He shook his head and looked at Malakai with hurt in his eyes. "Friends don't ask friends these kind of fucked up questions."

Malakai had killed more men than he cared to count but had never felt as horrible as he did right now. "Sorry, Joe, but I don't have the luxury of playing by normal friend rules. Hope you can get past me asking, but it had to be done."

"Yeah, I get it, I guess." Joe looked forlorn. "But having you ask me that question...you might just as well have taken a big ol' shit on my bar and then rubbed my face in it."

"I can still do that if it'll make you feel better."

"You're such an asshole."

"And then some." Malakai offered his hand. "Still friends?"

Joe hesitated and for a few seconds Malakai feared he had done irreparable damage to their relationship. But then the bartender shook his hand, clasping it firmly as he accepted the peace offering. "Sure, yeah, what the heck. You know I can't stay mad at anyone for very long."

"Except your ex-wife."

"Screw her."

"Not anymore, you're not."

"Like I said, you're an asshole." Joe reached into his pocket. "Here, I was gonna give this to you later, but I guess now's as good a time as any." He pulled out a piece of paper and handed it to Malakai. "Go to that address. Your birthday present is there."

"Joe..."

"Just humor me. If you get there and you don't like what you see, just turn around and come back. No hard feelings. But I think you'll like it."

"Joe, I can't."

Joe's eyes flashed hot sparks. "You throw that piece of paper away, I'm going to call you every name in the book, starting with a sorry piece of no-good shit. You dragged me back here, accused me of selling out a friend, and I took it like a man instead of smacking you upside the jaw like you deserved. Now, you want to make that up to me?"

"I said I was sorry."

"Apology and atonement are not the same thing. You want to be even-steven for that crap you just pulled, go to that address. If not, kiss my skinny black ass and find another bar."

Malakai grinned at him. "You're cute when you're mad."

"Nice try, but I don't swing that way," said Joe. "Now why are you still here?"

"I'm not. I'm on my way to a birthday party."

———

The establishment at the address Joe had provided had an actual name, but it might as well have been called the Come and Go Motel, because that's what people did here. A flophouse, pure and simple, a hooker's haven strikingly similar to the one in which Malakai temporarily resided. On the flophouse quality scale, this one might have been one step above his, but it was a really small step.

He steered the Corvette into a parking spot in front of Room #19 and killed the engine. Without the A/C running, the car's interior swiftly became stifling hot and he wished he had that Red Dog he had left on the bar back at Joe's. Maybe when he was finished here there would still be time to go back and get a cold one.

He sat in the car, stared at the room, and thought, *Joe, what the hell have you gotten me into?*

The curtains were closed but the lights were on. He occasionally glimpsed a vague silhouette of someone moving around inside. He let his combat senses probe his surroundings, but his primal instincts detected no threat of danger. That didn't change the fact that the whole situation was a bit weird. Then again, Joe was the one who had set this whole shenanigan up and you couldn't expect normalcy from a barkeep with a bow tie.

"Let's get this over with," Malakai muttered, climbing out of the Corvette and praying that it was still there when he finished tracking down this enigmatic birthday gift. He still sensed no immediate threat but couldn't shake the bad feeling bothering him. Maybe he was just too far outside his comfort zone. He didn't like surprises. He was an assassin, not a breed particularly known for appreciating the unexpected.

He walked up to the door and knocked. Then he stepped to the side in case someone shot through the door. Not that he expected anyone to shoot at him, but better safe than sorry. Catching a bullet in the belly would certainly ruin his birthday.

Nobody shot at him, but nobody answered either. But he could hear noises inside. Somebody was definitely in there. They just weren't opening the door. Then he heard what sounded like the sharp crack of flesh striking flesh, immediately followed by a woman's painful cry.

"Stop! Please! You're hurting me!" A feminine voice with a slight Japanese accent.

Malakai generally believed in minding his own business, but he couldn't just stand by while a woman got beat. He shucked out his gun and kicked in the door. The flimsy chain yielded to the force of the blow, links snapping apart. He surged into the room with his .45 at the ready, finger tight on the trigger.

He saw a gorgeous Japanese woman naked on the bed, wrists and ankles handcuffed to the bedposts. She did not look happy to be there, struggling against the stainless steel shackles. Raw, flaming welts striped her thighs, glowing a harsh, livid red. They had to hurt like hell; Malakai winced just looking at them.

A man stood beside the bed, shirtless, exposing a beach-bum tan and corded chest muscles with a tiger tattoo on his left pectoral. Malakai knew better than to judge a book by its cover, but this guy just looked like he enjoyed hurting people. Maybe it had something to do with the riding crop raised over his head as he prepared to strike the helpless woman again.

The man's head whipped around at Malakai's violent intrusion. "Hey!" he snapped. "Who the hell are you?"

"The guy who's about to put a bullet through your brain if you don't put that thing down," Malakai rasped.

Unbelievably, the man hesitated and seemed to be weighing his options. Apparently he had the body of a surfer, but the brains of someone who had been run over by the short bus one too many times.

"Seriously?" said Malakai. "You've got a piece of leather. I've got a gun. What's there to think about?"

The man nodded as if he had simply needed someone to put his position in the proper perspective and dropped the crop. It made a soft thump as it hit the carpet. "Listen," he said, "I don't know who you are, but I paid good money for this slut."

"Whore."

The man blinked at him. "Uh, what?"

"She's a whore," Malakai explained, "not a slut. A slut does it for free, a whore does it for money."

The man glared at him angrily. Whether it was because Malakai had interrupted his fun or had just made him feel stupid, it was hard to tell. Maybe both. "Well, thanks for the English lesson, Einstein. But slut, whore, or whatever you want to call her, I paid good money for this bitch, the kind of money that says I can do whatever the hell I want to her."

"Yeah?" said Malakai. "Well, I paid good money for this gun, the kind of money that says I can shoot whoever I want with it, and right now I'm thinking about shooting you in the balls. So do yourself a favor, shut your damn mouth, put your hands on your head, and walk toward me."

The man complied with all instructions, but as he walked toward Malakai, he kept yapping and whining. Probably some spoiled trust fund baby raised on a false sense of entitlement unaccustomed to not getting his way. "This is crap, man," he barked. "This is like entrapment or something. You a cop? Just what I don't frigging need, a night in jail." He stopped in front of Malakai.

"Turn around."

The man's face blanched. He suddenly seemed to realize that he had bigger things to worry about than an interrupted session with the hooker. "You're going to shoot me in the back of the head, aren't you?"

"If I wanted to shoot you, I would shoot you in the face. Now turn around."

Looking fearful, like it might be his last act on earth, the man obeyed. "Please," he whimpered. "Don't kill me. I have money. Just name your—"

Malakai bashed him with the butt of the .45 in the back of the head to shut him up. He half-expected the man's skull to sound hollow when he hit it. The guy slumped to the floor, unconscious, a lump starting to swell from the knockout blow. Malakai patted down his pockets and found the cuff key. He also found a handful of $100 bills that he helped himself to. Not because he needed it, but because he was feeling spiteful.

As he approached the woman shackled to the bed, he saw the welts on her legs blazed an angry red, neon stripes transgressing the otherwise unflawed smoothness of her skin. He quickly uncuffed her, trying his best not to look at her nakedness. But with such feminine perfection displayed so closely before him, keeping his eyes averted proved difficult. He stole enough glances to know that she put most centerfolds to shame. Definitely not the kind of woman you typically found working a sleaze-alley flophouse.

He wondered what tale of sorrow had brought her to a place like this. Whatever her story, no way it was a happy one. No fairytale ended with, *And then she lived happily ever after turning tricks in a fleabag motel.*

"Thank you," she said as the handcuffs fell away. She made no effort to cover herself as she massaged her wrists where the metal had bit into them.

"Got a name?" Malakai asked. He noticed her eyes were slightly larger than those of a typical Japanese woman and infused with a slight luminescence, a deep, shimmering brown nearly as dark as her jet-black hair.

"Of course," she said. "Everyone has a name." She started massaging her chafed ankles.

"That sounds like something from a fortune cookie."

She gave him a little smirk that he had to admit was kind of cute. "Fortune cookies are Chinese," she said. "I'm Japanese."

Malakai sighed. "Listen, lady, are you going to tell me your name or not?"

"My name is Shiomi."

"Great. Thanks for sharing. Now, Shiomi, we need to get out of here."

She slid off the bed. Her clothes were in a puddle of fabric on the floor and as she bent over to retrieve them, Malakai was treated to a view of her bare backside which could only be described as spectacular. No other adjective would suffice. He distracted himself by lifting the unconscious john onto the bed and preparing to handcuff him there.

"Wait," Shiomi said. "Roll him over." Apparently it didn't take long to put your clothes on when all you were wearing was a thin, spaghetti-strapped summer dress.

"Why do you want me to roll him over?"

Shiomi picked up the riding crop and slapped the hard leather against the palm of her hand. "Oh," she said, "just because."

Malakai shrugged. Facedown or face up, it didn't matter to him, as long as the guy was secured to the bed when they made their exit. He flipped the man over onto his stomach and shackled him to the bedposts with the handcuffs. He tossed the key into the far corner of the room.

"Thank you." Much to Malakai's surprise, Shiomi yanked the man's pants down and proceeded to viciously attack his exposed buttocks with the riding crop. She whipped the hard leather across the tender flesh over and over again until a patchwork of red-raw welts crisscrossed the man's ass. Malakai just stood there and watched, letting her get it out of her system. Besides, the guy totally had it coming.

When Shiomi finally stopped, she was breathing heavy but with a look of satisfaction on her face. "Take that, you bastard," she spat at her unconscious abuser. "How do you like it?"

Malakai arched an eyebrow at her. "Feel better?"

She seemed to think about it for a moment and then nodded. "Yes, actually, I do."

"Glad to hear it. Can we go now?"

———

He hadn't been gone long enough for the Corvette to be carjacked, though a pack of hoodlums across the street were eyeballing it appreciatively. When he exited the room with Shiomi in tow, they wolf-whistled and called out, "Hey, man, nice ride!" Malakai wasn't sure if they were referring to the car or Shiomi.

Once they were in the Corvette, Malakai wasted no time in putting some distance between them and the motel. He wasn't concerned about leaving the man handcuffed in the room. He would be found soon enough and it was unlikely he would go to the police and report being attacked by a hooker he hired. But if he had a wife or girlfriend, it was going to be real hard to explain those welts on his backside.

Thinking of welts made him remember that Shiomi had been whipped herself. "You should probably see a doctor," he said. "I'll take you to the emergency room."

She waved away his concern. "No need for that. Just stop by a store and pick up some iodine and gauze."

"I've got that stuff back at my room."

"Take me there then, if you don't mind." She smiled at him. The kind of smile designed to make the heart soft and other parts of the male anatomy not soft. "And by the way, happy birthday."

"You were my present from Joe?"

Shiomi nodded. "I work out of that motel a lot, so that's where I had Joe send you. That guy you busted up, he's one of my regulars, but tonight he wanted to switch things up and go all kinky."

"You actually let him handcuff you to the bed?" It was a foreign concept to Malakai. He would rather suck the snot out of a dead skunk's nostrils than voluntarily submit to shackles.

"No, I told him kink wasn't my thing. But instead of taking 'no' for an answer, he punched me in the jaw and the next thing I know, I'm cuffed to the bed and he's flogging me like a bad mule. Lucky for me you came along when you did." She gave him another one of those delicious smiles. "Maybe you're my guardian angel."

"Trust me, lady, I'm no angel."

"Maybe not, but you're no devil either."

"You don't know that. I could be the wickedest son of a bitch you've ever met."

"I know men," she replied.

He gave her a sideways glance. "Is that supposed to be funny?"

"No." She said it quietly and with just a hint of pain. "No, it's not funny at all." She turned her head and stared out the window as the city rushed by. The remainder of the drive passed in silence. Someone else might have found it uncomfortable, but silence suited Malakai just fine.

When they got to his motel room, Malakai steered Shiomi into the bathroom where she lowered the toilet lid and sat down while he rummaged up some iodine and gauze from his duffel bag. As a gun for hire, he couldn't run to the doctor every time he sustained a wound, so he always kept basic first aid supplies on hand.

Crouching down in front of her, he soaked some gauze with iodine and began patting down the welts on her legs. Even covered in red stripes, they were very nice legs. She winced when the iodine hit one of the worst welts and Malakai quickly pulled back.

"It's okay," Shiomi said. "Just stings a little. Keep going and let's get this over with."

Malakai went back to work for a few moments, then said, "Don't take this the wrong way, but if you want me to clean the rest, you'll have to raise your dress. Or I can step out and you can do it yourself."

Shiomi gave him a smile that was both sweet and sultry. With deliberate, exaggerated sensuality, she slowly pulled her dress up until her inner thighs came into view.

To Malakai, the room suddenly seemed very, very warm.

When he reached out with the gauze and iodine, Shiomi put her hand on top of his and began slowly sliding it up her leg.

"What are you doing?" Malakai asked as she guided his fingers higher and higher, one slow inch at a time.

"My job," Shiomi said and the huskiness in her voice almost sounded sincere.

Malakai looked into her beautiful dark eyes for a moment and then abruptly jerked his hand away from the tantalizing skin just beneath his fingertips. "I don't have time for this."

He exited the bathroom and sat down on the edge of the bed as irritation and arousal warred within him. More accurately, his arousal irritated him, because it was not normal for him to be attracted to someone who had been paid to smile nice and ride him good. He killed for money so he wasn't one to judge, but hookers just weren't his thing. That said, he was a man like any other, and Shiomi was one of the most beautiful women he had laid eyes on in a long time. Maybe ever.

So what the hell is she doing as a whore?

Didn't matter. It was none of his business. He grabbed the remote and flipped through TV stations as Shiomi emerged from the bathroom and came toward him. He pretended to be engrossed by a commercial. It took him a moment to realize it was an advertisement about erectile dysfunction. He groaned inwardly.

Sometimes God had a sick sense of humor. He deliberately refused to look at Shiomi.

She forced the issue by kneeling in front of him, blocking his view of the television, practically willing his eyes to meet hers. She looked at him and he looked at her and all was quiet for several moments. Then she softly asked, "Don't you like me?"

Malakai sighed. "I don't even know you," he said. "You're a beautiful woman, no doubt about that, and most men would probably give their right arm to be with you."

"Most men...but not you."

"Right."

"Why not?"

"No offense," he said, "but you're a working girl. Not my type."

"Working girl," she echoed bitterly. "You mean whore."

"Your term, not mine," Malakai said, "but yeah. I'm not pointing any fingers because believe me, I'm no saint. But the fact remains that you were paid to let me touch you like that. You were paid to give yourself to me."

"So?" Shiomi sounded both defiant and defensive. "Happens all the time. Oldest profession in the book. Ever since Adam popped a tent in his fig leaf, Eve started figuring out a way to make him pay for it." She stared at him intensely. "I didn't choose this life, you know. I didn't wake up one morning and say, 'Hey, you know what, I think I'll become a whore.' But shit happens."

Malakai sensed her desperate need for him to understand. "Shit happens is a concept I'm all too familiar with," he said, repressing the memories that wanted to surge forth like demons loosed from a cage. "Like I said, I'm no saint, but my life doesn't have room for a woman and even if it did, I wouldn't be interested unless that woman wanted to be with me. Paying for it just isn't my style."

"How quaint," Shiomi said. "A man with morals."

"More like personal preferences."

"That's fine...uh..." She let out a laugh. "Hey, I don't even know your name."

"Malakai."

"Strange name."

"My father had a thing for the minor prophets."

"Well, Malakai, your morals or personal preferences or whatever you want to call them create a couple of problems for me. For starters, I've been paid to sleep with you. Apparently that's not going to happen, so I took money for services that I'm not going to provide."

"Keep it. I broke the deal, not you."

"Thanks," she said. "But the second problem is, you might very well have saved my life tonight and the only way I have to repay you is this." She stood up and let the thin straps of her dress fall from her shoulders. The garment hissed silkily against her skin as it slithered to the floor. Almost against his will, his eyes drank in her naked beauty.

Malakai felt his body instinctively responding, but he refused to be a slave to his lusts. He controlled his body, not the other way around. "Shiomi," he said. "No. Just...don't."

She put her hands on his shoulders and moved in even closer. Heat radiated off her skin, pulling at him like a seductive magnet. "Why don't you shut up and kiss me?" she said softly as she leaned in, lips wet and inviting.

Malakai pulled his head back, retreating from her advance. "Why won't you take no for an answer?"

She paused with her lips just a few inches from his. "It's just a kiss, Malakai."

He didn't move further away from her, but he didn't move closer either. "A kiss is never just a kiss."

They stayed that way for several long, pulsing moments as her eyes searched his face, seeking some sign of relenting on his part. Malakai made sure she didn't find it, keeping his features a stony mask that would have been the envy of a world champion poker player. At last Shiomi withdrew with a heavy sigh. "Fine, I'll just have to find another way to repay you."

"There's no need," he said.

"I pay my debts."

"You don't owe me anything."

She slipped on her dress and headed for the door. "That's not for you to decide." She stood with her hand on the knob. "I guess I'll be leaving now," she said, and then paused, as if hoping he would tell her to wait, call her back, ask her not to go.

But Malakai didn't do any of those things. All he asked was, "Do you need a ride somewhere?"

She sighed again, a lonely sound tinged with desperation and laced with despair. "No," she said. "I'll call a cab. Thanks anyway." She opened the door and walked out into the night.

Malakai sat on the bed for a long time after Shiomi left, listening to one voice in his head tell him what a noble man he was and another voice tell him that he was a complete idiot. He finally silenced them both by taking a cold shower.

Afterwards, drying off with a towel that closely resembled rough-grit sandpaper, he pushed all thoughts of the gorgeous prostitute from his mind as he began mental preparations for tomorrow morning's hit on Jim Abbott.

CHAPTER 8

DAWN FOUND Malakai moving into position to intercept his quarry at the Tampa International Airport. He parked the Chevy Tahoe he had rented—he would have to trail Abbott from the airport and the Corvette was far too conspicuous—and walked into the main terminal, the roar of jets overhead little more than white noise in the background. Pedestrian traffic was fairly light this early in the day; the elbow-to-elbow congestion would come later. But by then he would be long gone, his bank account fattened, the world population reduced by one treasonous ex-Marine.

Inside the terminal, he checked the monitors and confirmed that Jim Abbott's flight was scheduled to touch down at 4:39 a.m. He glanced at his watch. It was 4:05 a.m.

He made his way to the waiting area just outside the security checkpoint and leaned against the wall, blending in with his surroundings like a human chameleon, just another person waiting for an incoming flight to arrive.

He deliberately avoided making eye contact with Abbott when the man walked by in the wave of disembarking passengers, using only his peripheral vision to identify his target. Many people possessed an innate sense of when they were being watched, a survival instinct inherited from prehistoric ancestors, and Malakai did not want to tip Abbott off that he was a target. He let several seconds pass before he pushed away from the wall and began tailing the ex-Marine, following him at a distance as he made his way out of the terminal and into the parking garage. According to Malakai's intel, Abbott's brother had left a car parked in the garage for him to use, saving Abbott the hassle of having to rent one. Malakai would bet dollars to dimes that there was a gun stashed in the glove compartment or under the seat. Abbott would want access to a firearm and since he couldn't carry on the plane, having his brother leave a weapon in the car would be the easiest way to arm himself.

The garage was less crowded than the terminal, so Malakai widened the gap between him and Abbott; far enough back to avoid detection but close enough to not lose his prey. Abbott acted a bit twitchy, but Malakai chalked that up to nerves. The man gave no sign of having detected his tail.

Abbott's vehicle was a nondescript blue Ford Taurus, parked one level above where Malakai had parked the Tahoe. Concealed behind a concrete pillar, he watched Abbott load his luggage into the trunk with the exception of a black briefcase that he put in the front seat with him. Malakai felt reasonably confident in assuming the briefcase contained the blackmail material.

He dropped down to the next level and started the Tahoe. He cranked up the A/C and waited. Less than two minutes later, Abbott drove by, following the large white arrows toward the exit. Malakai took out his FNX-45 and set it on the passenger seat for easy access, then pulled out after him.

He followed the Taurus out of the shadows of the parking garage into the orange light of dawn, merging with the traffic flowing onto the Howard Frankland, the long bridge that spanned Tampa Bay and connected the city of Tampa to St. Petersburg.

Early morning traffic was light on the four lane highway, which made maneuvering easier, but tailing more difficult. They passed a green road sign that said "St. Petersburg 10 miles" as Abbott steered the Taurus into the far right lane. Malakai stayed one lane over and kept a couple cars between them. He glanced out the window and saw morning fog swirling on the waters of the bay. It would soon be scorched away by the rising sun.

He had considered hitting Abbott right in the parking garage, but the presence of too many surveillance cameras had nixed that idea. Not a problem; he would simply follow his target until an opportunity presented itself. The mandate to recover the photos of Senator Olander complicated things. Without that mission component, he could just pull up next to Abbott on the highway, pop a bullet in his temple, and watch the car crash into the concrete barriers, maybe even flipping off the bridge into the ocean below. It would be a spectacular kill, but it wouldn't put the photos in his possession.

Up ahead, the taillights of the Taurus flashed red as

Abbott braked hard. The move was so totally unexpected that before Malakai could react, he found himself side by side with his target. When he looked over and saw Abbott aiming a gun out the car window, he realized he had been made. He didn't know how—maybe he made a mistake or maybe he had been betrayed again—but right now it didn't matter.

He stomped on his brakes and grabbed his .45 at the same time, but not before Abbott gunned a trio of rounds through the passenger side window. The glass shattered into glittering cubes that the wind whipped away. The bullets all missed their mark, but not by much. He probably could have stuck his tongue out and given them a lick as they flew past his face. He gritted his teeth and refused to think about his own mortality.

Malakai steered with his left hand and hefted the .45 with his right. The time for stealth was over. No more foreplay—time to hit and hit hard. Recovering the photos had just been downgraded to secondary concern. Survival was now his primary objective.

Malakai accelerated up alongside the Taurus, gun raised, aiming out the window. He got Abbott in his sights and pulled the trigger. As the .45 bucked and spat a spent casing into the back seat, Abbott ducked forward. The bullet scored the air where his head had been a heartbeat before.

"Shit!" Malakai adjusted his aim, seeking to regain target acquisition.

Abbott reacted swiftly, proving he was no slouch when it came to combat instincts. He jerked the wheel to the left and slammed the Taurus into the Tahoe. Since the SUV was the heavier vehicle, Malakai maintained control with no trouble, but the impact threw off his aim. Metal crunched and sparks flew and when the two vehicles parted company, Abbott fired a wild shot and got lucky.

Malakai jerked as the bullet struck him in the left shoulder. Blood spattered across the windshield. It looked like little red raindrops, except they were on the inside of the glass. It hurt like hell but he gritted his teeth and fought through the pain. Wasn't like he had a choice.

The two vehicles hurtled down the highway, weaving around the traffic, exchanging gunfire. Windows imploded and bullets gouged holes in body-work, but neither man could score a kill-shot. Malakai wished he had brought heavier firepower. Something with full auto capability. Or a rocket launcher.

Abbott suddenly punched the gas and spurted ahead, tossing off another blind shot at the same time. The bullet tore through the Tahoe's windshield and blew apart the top of the steering wheel. Fragments peppered Malakai's startled face. He couldn't believe it. One lucky bullet could be chalked up to pure chance. Two lucky bullets and it became clear the gods of war were smiling down on Abbott and giving him high-fives.

"Fuck you," he growled.

He slammed his foot down on the gas and swerved around a slow-moving Hyundai, catching a glimpse of a petrified old lady white-knuckling the wheel as he flew by in a banged up, broken-glassed, bullet-holed vehicle that looked like it had served two tours of duty in Iraq. He felt bad for scaring the crap out of her, but at least she would have a whopper of a story to tell the grand-kids later.

The longer this high-speed firefight dragged on, the

greater the odds of an innocent getting caught in the crossfire. The game needed to end, right now, and Malakai made a move toward checkmate. He whipped the Tahoe across the lane in front of the Hyundai and directly behind the Taurus. He saw Abbott glance in his rearview mirror, but before the ex-Marine could perform an evasive maneuver, Malakai fired a round through his own shattered windshield. The heavy .45 caliber round punched through the back window of the Taurus and smashed into the back of Abbot's skull. The impact slammed him forward to slump over the steering wheel, most of his face splattered across the dashboard.

Malakai swerved out from behind the Taurus as it strayed into the breakdown lane, Abbott's dead foot on the gas keeping it charging forward at full speed. Up ahead, some unlucky driver was changing a flat tire on his Camaro. He saw the Taurus careening toward him. With no other options, he threw himself off the bridge and into the waters of Tampa Bay, narrowing avoiding being crushed.

The Taurus crunched into the Camaro, the latter acting as a launching ramp for the former. It looked like a perfectly executed stunt in an action movie, except this was real life and there was a dead body in the car instead of a stunt driver.

The Taurus sailed into the air, barrel-rolled, and slammed down on its roof in a shower of sparks. Momentum caused it to tumble end over end down the highway before finally coming to a stop upside down, a trail of broken debris strewn in its wake.

Malakai pulled over onto the shoulder, quickly slapped a fresh magazine into the FNX, then exited the Tahoe and jogged back to the wreckage. Torn electrical wires snapped and sizzled but the fuel tank appeared to be intact, so there was no danger of fire or explosion.

That would change in just a minute.

He ducked down, reached inside the vehicle, and retrieved the black briefcase. Other than some blood spatter, it seemed none the worse for wear for having taken a ride in a speeding, jumping, flipping, tumbling car.

Malakai walked back to the Tahoe, then turned and pumped a half-dozen bullets into the Taurus' gas tank, spilling fuel all over the sparking wires. Moments later the smashed car burst into flames. Not the mush-rooming fireball of a Hollywood movie, but the kind of burn-baby-burn conflagration that would cook Abbott's corpse into a charred mess. Not to mention make anyone who knew about the blackmail photos of Senator Olander assume they had been destroyed in the blaze.

Back in the Tahoe, Malakai opened the briefcase and then pressed a hand over the bullet wound in his shoulder as he quickly scanned the photographs. He needed to get the hell away from here, but not before he made sure he had the right pictures.

He flipped through the glossy Polaroids. Yeah, no doubt these were the right ones. They weren't quite as bad as they were rumored to be—no donkey to be found —but definitely featured a much younger Paula Olander engaged in some hardcore bondage stuff that no female senator would ever want made public.

He tossed the photos back into the briefcase. His eyes had suffered enough.

He closed the briefcase and stuffed it down into the front passenger foot well. Those photos were bargaining chips and in his line of work, you could never have too many bargaining chips.

Especially when you keep getting burned, he thought. Probably a morbid choice of metaphor with Abbott cooking in his own juices just forty yards away, but oh well.

Other cars were stopping, the rubber-neckers and gore-ghouls pulling over to get their fix. Probably some kindhearted Good Samaritans too, if those still existed in modern day society. By now someone would have dialed 911 on their cell and the police would be inbound.

Time to hit the road.

Malakai swung the Tahoe back onto the highway and drove away. Someone probably snapped a picture of his license plate, but no matter; he had rented it using one of the multiple aliases maintained for him by the Company. Besides, he planned on ditching the vehicle in the very near future.

Once he was rolling south again, Malakai called Father Thomas on his cell phone. The ex-priest would probably be pissed at being awakened at the crack of dawn, but given the situation, Malakai really didn't care. Actually, even not given the situation, he wouldn't have cared.

Father Thomas couldn't have been sleeping, because he answered on just the second ring, with his customary lack of pleasantry. "Yeah?"

Malakai got right down to business. "The job went sideways. You have any friends in the St. Pete area?"

"Let me answer a question with a question: is the job finished and do you have the photos?"

"It's finished but the photos were destroyed."

"Damn it, man, I told you we wanted those photos recovered!" Malakai could almost feel his handler's anger coming through the cellular signal.

"Too bad," he snapped. "Abbott knew I was coming. You know what that means? I was burned again. That shit is starting to get real old. I managed to take him out but there were complications that need to be addressed and I mean right fucking now."

"What kind of complications?"

"I'm southbound on the Howard Frankland in a vehicle that looks like it's been through a war. I sustained some personal damage too."

"How bad?"

"Shoulder wound. I'll live, but I need to ditch this ride ASAP and get back to home turf."

"Take the first exit off the bridge and stick to side roads as best you can," Father Thomas said.

"No shit, Tom. This ain't my first rodeo."

"You know where the Clearwater airport is?"

"I'll find it."

"About five miles past the airport, there's a small farm, owned by a guy named Orville. He'll be standing by with a chopper to fly you back to Miami. Good enough?"

"Let's hope so." Malakai terminated the call.

———

The early morning sun peeked through the branches of the palm trees thirty minutes later as Malakai bounced his way up a deeply rutted tractor lane of a driveway, steam gushing from the Chevy's radiator. He spotted a large wooden barn up ahead, the doors open, a middle-aged man wearing a straw hat and denim coveralls standing outside. The man motioned for him to drive the Tahoe into the barn.

Malakai pulled in and killed the engine, which struck him as an act of mercy, since the punished motor was about to die anyway. He climbed out of the vehicle as the man shut the barn doors and then turned to him, hand extended.

"Howdy. Name's Orville." His drawl sounded more Texas cowboy than Florida farmer.

Malakai shook his hand and said, "Better for both of us if you don't know my name, but I do appreciate the help."

Orville nodded. "No problem. I've done a few of these cloak and dagger rides for Tom and I've learned not to expect much in the way of information, which suits me just fine. Far as I'm concerned, a man's business is a man's business."

Malakai rotated his shoulder, testing the limits of the bullet wound, wincing slightly at the pain. Wasn't his first time getting shot, but it always hurt like hell. At least it was a clean through-and-through, no shattered bone to deal with. "How long have you known Tom?" he asked.

"Met him 'bout a year or so before he left the priesthood. Me and my family used to attend mass at his church. My son was even an altar boy there for a while."

"You're the first person I've ever met that knew Tom in his former life. You know why he stopped being a priest?"

Orville stared at him sternly. "I know exactly why he stopped being a priest, but I'll be damned if I'm gonna tell you, 'cause like I said, a man's business is a man's business, nobody else's. If Tom wanted you to know why he traded the collar for a gun, then you'd know. But you don't, so he doesn't."

Orville's tone made it clear that further discussion on the matter would not be appreciated. Malakai decided to let it go. Not like he had a choice, other than sticking a gun in the farmer's face and demanding answers and that seemed ill-advised since he needed Orville to give him a ride back to Miami. "Fair enough," he said. He walked around to the passenger side of the Tahoe and retrieved the black suitcase. "Now, where's this chopper of yours?"

Orville jerked a thumb toward the rear of the barn. "'Round back."

Malakai followed the farmer out the back door to where a chopper squatted on a patch of sunbaked dirt. The bird was an old Bell UH-1 Iroquois, commonly referred to as a "Huey", and looked like it might have been the last slick out of Saigon back in 1975.

Orville seemed to sense his thoughts. "She looks rough," he said, "but that's just cosmetics. Trust me, her mechanics are tip-top." He patted the engine cowl affectionately. The metal sported some gouges, probably from North Vietnamese antiaircraft guns. "This ol' gal survived one of the dirtiest wars this country has ever seen, she'll survive a quick trip to Miami."

"I'll take your word for it."

"Ever been up in a chopper?"

"Yeah, a year or so ago. Took some HALO training."

"High altitude, low opening jumps ain't no joke,"

Orville said. "Guess that means you aren't afraid of heights."

"Not in the least," said Malakai. Blood dripped from the hole in his shoulder and spattered the dust.

Orville eyeballed the red droplets. "Since you seem to have sprung a leak, I gotta ask, are you gonna bleed out and die in my chopper, sonny?"

"Bleed, yes. Die, no."

Orville looked at him with grudging respect. "Tough guy, hey? Good enough. Get in and let's get gone."

Malakai climbed into the chopper, wincing in pain, which intensified as the natural anesthetic of shock and adrenaline continued to wear off. He leaned his head back against the seat and closed his eyes as Orville fired up the bird. He kept them closed even when he felt the chopper lift off into the morning sky and bank south toward Miami.

CHAPTER 9

MALAKAI UNLOCKED his motel room door and stepped inside, thinking about a shower, stitching up the holes in his shoulder, and catching some sleep. Those thoughts all went to hell in a heartbeat when he hit the lights and saw someone standing in the middle of the room.

He dropped the briefcase and drew his .45 in about a second flat. Another second and recognition set in. Good thing too, since the trigger was about an ounce away from breakpoint. He lowered the gun but didn't put it away. Not yet. Not until he had some answers.

"Shiomi, what the hell are you doing here?" he demanded. "I almost killed you."

The gorgeous Japanese hooker seemed unfazed by the threat of the gun. "I brought you a present," she said, pointing to a gift-box on the dresser, complete with a bright red bow adorning the lid. It looked ludicrously out of place in the cheap, skanky motel room.

"How did you get in here?"

"In my line of work, you pick up a trick or two. No

pun intended." She smiled. "One of my regulars taught me to pick locks. There's not too many doors that can keep me out."

Satisfied no immediate threat existed, Malakai flicked on the gun's safety. "Yeah, well, there's some doors you walk through, you catch a bullet." He pulled back his jacket to holster the .45, exposing his blood-soaked shirt in the process.

"Oh my God!" Shiomi gasped. "You're bleeding."

"Yeah, that happens sometimes when you get shot."

"You need to go to the hospital." She seemed genuinely concerned.

Malakai shook his head. "Not happening. Hospitals have to report all gunshot wounds to the cops and that is one headache I don't need right now."

"Well, we have to do *something*. Maybe we should take one of your bullets apart, put the gunpowder on the wound, and then burn it shut."

"You've been watching too many movies," Malakai said. "Do you know how to use a needle?"

"I'm not a junkie."

"A *sewing* needle."

"Oh. Sorry." She smiled. "Yeah, sure. Well, I mean, kind of."

"Good enough for me," he said. "The bullet went through clean, no bone. I'm gonna hit the shower, get this blood off me, then you can stitch me up."

She looked uncertain. "Listen, I'm not so sure..."

Malakai cut her off. "You said you wanted to repay me, right? Do this thing for me and we're even."

Shiomi hesitated, then nodded reluctantly. "Okay, but I'm no Martha Stewart, so you'll probably have a hell of a scar."

Malakai headed for the bathroom. "I've got lots of scars. You get used to them after a while."

———

Malakai turned the faucet handle until the water was just shy of scalding and then spent twenty minutes standing under the spray, letting the water pound his flesh with soothing heat. Surprisingly good water pressure for a cheap flophouse, neither a firehose nor a trickle but a happy medium in between. He grimaced as the spray hit the dark, ugly bullet holes in his shoulder, rinsing away the blood so that it spiraled down the rust-spackled drain between his feet.

He was startled when the stall door opened and Shiomi stepped into the shower with him. She had brought a bottle of Jack Daniels, a needle, and some thread. What she had not brought was her clothes. He was struck once again by her naked, exotic beauty and stared a little longer than was polite, unable to pull his eyes away from her stunning body.

He finally found the ability to form coherent words again and asked, "What are you doing?"

She smiled and if there wasn't a hint of seduction in the sensual curve of her red-glossed lips, then he was no judge of people. "You said you wanted me to stitch you up."

"Yeah, after I got out of the shower." It was getting hot in here and it had nothing to do with the steam. Malakai tried to keep his eyes locked on hers, but they betrayed him with a mind of their own, dipping down to the kind of perfect breasts that proved there was a God. Shower spray beaded her silky smooth skin.

"Easier this way," she said. "The water will keep the wound clear of blood so I can see what I'm doing."

"I'm not sure this is such a good idea." He had fought a lot of battles in his life, but few harder than the battle to keep his gaze up right now. It felt like his eyes were made of metal and her nude body was a magnet.

"Relax," she said. "It's not like you haven't already seen me naked."

She kind of had a point. Difference was, the first time he had seen her naked, she hadn't been standing in the shower with him. It definitely changed the dynamic. He really needed to think about something else. He glanced at the bottle of Jack Daniels and asked, "Where'd you get the moonshine?"

"Liquor store around the corner."

"Didn't know they were open this early."

"They're not." She smiled wickedly. "Told you I was good at picking locks."

She stepped behind him and leaned over to set the needle and thread down on the soap ledge. He glanced over his shoulder and glimpsed her perfect heart-shaped ass with rivulets of hot water streaming off the satin skin. He tore his eyes away as desire pounded in his veins, a carnal rhythm putting his willpower to the ultimate test.

If Shiomi noticed his internal struggle, she didn't comment. She twisted the cap off the whiskey and said, "This is going to sting a little." Then she poured the booze over the top of Malakai's shoulder, letting it run down both the front and back so that the cleansing burn seared through both the entry and exit holes.

Malakai clenched his teeth. "Holy *shit*, that hurts."

"Yeah, that's what I meant when I said 'this is going to sting a little'."

Shiomi put down the bottle and picked up the needle and thread. Malakai heard her take a deep breath and then felt the prick of the needle and tug of the stitches as she got to work, sewing up the exit wound with surprising speed and grace.

When she finished, she leaned back to study her handiwork. "Not bad." She sounded pleased with herself. "You're lucky the bullet didn't mushroom or that hole would be the size of a fist."

"Yeah, that's me," Malakai said. "Luckiest son of a bitch in the world."

"Okay, turn around so I can stitch up the front."

Malakai hesitated. Turning around would let her see his body's natural arousal to her nearness and nudity. Talk about an awkward moment. But he needed the wound stitched, so he didn't have much choice. *Just get it over with,* he told himself.

With a deep sigh of resignation, he turned around.

Shiomi didn't even pretend not to look; her eyes immediately dipped below his waist. With a soft smile, she said, "Mmmmm, you really *are* lucky."

Malakai kept his own eyes straight ahead. "Will you please just get on with it?"

She stepped in close and began sewing, her breasts inadvertently—or maybe not so inadvertently—grazing his solar plexus as she worked. Malakai had thought he couldn't get any more worked up. He had thought wrong. He took a deep, shuddering breath.

Shiomi paused and looked down. "That's perfectly normal, you know," she said with a smirk.

"Thanks," Malakai replied wryly. "I wasn't aware of that."

She finished stitching him up, then turned around to set down the needle and thread. When she bent over, he got another look at her perfect, water-glistened ass. He could feel his self-control rapidly crumbling around the edges. He let out an audible groan.

She stood up and faced him again, moving in close until their bodies were pressed together. Her hands rested on his hips as she brushed her lips against his in a ghost of a kiss and said, "I gave Joe back his money."

Malakai knew he should back away, but he couldn't. He wasn't sure any man in his position could. Her stunning beauty and intoxicating presence worked in tandem to batter down his resistance. "I told you to keep the money," he said, "and I meant it."

"I wanted to see you again," Shiomi said, "and the money seemed to be a problem for you."

"Why would you want to see me again?"

She took a half-step back so she could look up into his eyes. She stood in the shower spray and stared at him for several long moments before she said, "There's just something about you, Malakai. I look at you and for the first time in a long time I see somebody who might actually understand my scars." She moved into him again, lifting her arms around his neck. "Last night you said you only wanted to be with someone who wants you. Well, *I* want you, Malakai. I want to be with you."

Malakai looked at her and while he saw no scars on her flesh, he could see the emotional scars behind her eyes, the scars on the inside. And he knew better than most that those scars are the ones that hurt the most. The fact that he could see those scars let him know that she was making herself vulnerable, exposing herself to him in a way that had nothing to do with naked skin. Regretting the words even as he spoke them, he said, "I don't have room in my life for a woman right now."

"Who said anything about life?" she asked breathlessly as her lips moved toward his. "Right now we're just talking about today." She kissed him urgently, with a need that went far beyond simple desire.

Malakai stopped fighting. Maybe he needed this as much as she did. He surrendered to the moment, the last vestiges of his willpower falling away like chiseled stone. He leaned into her kiss with a fierce passion that surprised even him and she returned it hungrily. Whatever she needed from him, whatever she took, it was clear in that moment that she would pay him back in kind. He clutched her close and let his hands caress her succulent curves. She threw her head back and let the shower spray rain down on her face as he licked the water from the hollow of her throat.

His mouth found hers again as he crushed her against the wall of the shower. She gasped and shuddered as they moved together with reckless abandon, two wounded souls in communion, both desperate to find in each other something they could not even define.

———

Hours later, they laid in bed, two shadows pressed together, rumpled sheets entwined around them. The air conditioner rattled like it was in its death throes as it struggled to blow cool air over their sweat-slicked bodies.

Shiomi nestled her head on his shoulder, fingers lightly tracing a knife scar on his chest, just below the collarbone. A souvenir from an assignment gone wrong in Israel. He'd been tortured by a rogue Mossad agent stealing and selling rare religious artifacts on the black market to fund a Hamas terrorist cell. Gabriel Asher had pulled his ass out of the fire, terminating the Mossad motherfucker and literally carrying Malakai on his back for three-quarters of a mile to the extraction point.

Ah, the good ol' days, he thought wryly.

"Thank you," Shiomi said softly, pulling him back to the present. "It's been a long time since I was with someone who didn't treat me like a whore."

Malakai considered telling her how he had got that particular scar, but decided not to. So many damn scars, each with their own story. "If you don't like your life," he said, "change it."

"It's not that easy."

"Sure it is. Just stop turning tricks."

"Oh, it's that simple, is it?" She lifted her head and looked at him. "Could you just stop assassinating people?"

"I never said I was an assassin."

"You don't have to," she replied. "The evidence is there and I'm smart enough to put it together."

"What evidence?"

"The gun, the lonely existence, all the scars, the bullet hole in your shoulder."

"You've got it all wrong," said Malakai. "I sell Girl Scout cookies for a living. I got this bullet hole because some asshole was pissed off that I was out of Samoas."

"I'm being serious, Malakai."

"Fine," he said. "Not that I'm confirming anything, but if I am what you think I am, then the answer is yes, I could stop if I wanted to. Difference is, I don't want to stop. You do."

"I never said I wanted to stop hooking."

"You don't have to. The evidence is there and I'm smart enough to put it together."

"Jerk," she muttered, but she said it with a smile and without anger.

He kissed her forehead. "I can see it in your eyes, Shiomi. You want out."

"So let's get out together," she said. "I'll stop turning tricks if you stop taking contracts."

Malakai gave her a look. "Are you propositioning me?"

She smiled, that intoxicating mix of mischief and seduction. "Maybe." Her tone was the very definition of coy.

Malakai pulled her close. "Maybe we should find out if we're still compatible," he said, giving her a wicked grin of his own.

She laughed and gently pushed him away. "Maybe later. Right now I want to give you your present."

She climbed out of bed and Malakai admired the sway of her hips as she retrieved the gift-box from the dresser. He wondered if she practiced moving like that or if it just came natural. She brought the gift-box back to the bed and placed it on his lap as he sat up, bunching the pillows behind him for back support.

He put his hands on each side of the box and looked at her. "You really didn't need to get me anything."

"Just shut up and open it," she said.

"Well, since you asked so nicely." He smiled as he

removed the lid, reached into the box, and lifted out a glass bowl with two red fish in it. They flitted around just inches from his hand. His smile instantly vanished like a cobweb in a hurricane as he let out a horrible cry and dropped the bowl. It tumbled from his grasp and spilled its contents onto the bed. Malakai started freaking out as the fish flopped on his lap.

"Get 'em off me! GET 'EM OFF ME!"

His reaction stunned Shiomi. In a panicked voice she asked, "What is it? What's wrong?"

"The fish! The fucking fish! Get 'em off me!"

"Okay, okay!" Shiomi hurriedly scooped both fish back into the bowl, still partially filled with water. The traumatized fish darted frantically around the perimeter of their glass prison. They looked even more goggle-eyed than usual.

Not that Malakai cared. No matter how trauma-tized they were, their traumatization didn't hold a candle to his. He sat on the bed, damn near hyperventi-lating, his breath fast and shallow as his pulse revved into the redline zone.

Shiomi touched his shoulder and said, "Malakai, talk to me. What's wrong?"

He didn't say anything. Too busy trying to get his heartrate under control. The blood pounded so hard in his veins that it felt like they were going to rupture like over-pressurized hydraulic hoses.

She shook him and she wasn't gentle about it. Not quite rough enough to shake him like a rag doll, but a man with weaker neck muscles probably would have looked like a bobble-head. "Damn it, Malakai, talk to me or so help me God, I will call an ambulance, the hell with your gunshot wound."

He believed her. He had already figured out that she wasn't the bluffing type. He had to tell her something. He decided to go with the truth.

A shudder racked him as he muttered, "Fucking fish." He could feel beads of sweat dappling his forehead. He was not the easily embarrassed type, but it crossed his mind that he was making one hell of a lousy impression.

Shiomi looked confused. "They're Red Fire Guppies. What about them?"

"I'm ichthyophobic."

Her confused look did not go away. "And what exactly does that mean?"

"It means fish scare the shit out of me."

Shiomi stared at him as if he had just announced that he rode a pink dragon to work and collected unicorn testicles for a hobby. "They're just guppies," she said. "Harmless as a butterfly. You're acting like I gave you a barracuda."

Malakai was starting to come down from his fear-induced burst of adrenalin. His pulse wasn't exactly normal yet, but it no longer gave a NASCAR engine a run for its money. "You could have given me a baby minnow and I would have reacted the same way."

"That doesn't make any sense."

"Yeah," Malakai said, "that's why they call it a phobia. It's an irrational fear. Doesn't change the fact that me and fish are not friends."

"But why?" Shiomi asked. "Did something happen?"

"Yeah, you could say that." Malakai held up his left hand, the one missing the pinkie. "A fish ate my finger, that's what happened. I was only nine years old." He lowered his hand. "My friend's father collected exotic fish. He had a big tank with Red Bellied piranha in it. He fed them live mice and being a young boy, I thought that was just the coolest thing, watching those fish tear into that little mouse." Malakai's eyes started going out of focus, the classic thousand yard stare, as he relived the memories.

The piranha tank...a loud man with a big, jiggling beer belly and receding hair line and breath that stinks of cheap booze...the man laughing as he dangles a white mouse over the water ... the needle-toothed fish darting about in ravenous anticipation...the squeaking mouse tumbling into the tank...the rodent being ripped to pieces right in front of Malakai's wide-eyed face on the other side of the glass...

Shiomi was wide-eyed as well, sitting next to him on the bed in rapt attention, like a little girl being told the world's worst bedtime story.

"One afternoon my friend's father got drunk off his ass," Malakai continued. "He sees me standing by the tank and launches into this sermon about how in the Amazon jungle, young boys are required to swim with piranha as a rite of passage into manhood or some shit like that. Then he grabbed my hand and stuck it in the tank."

"Oh my God!" Shiomi gasped.

"Trust me, God wasn't there," Malakai said with a trace of bitterness. "For some reason, the piranha went for my pinkie first. I screamed and screamed but he just laughed and held my hand under the water while the fish chewed my finger off."

Malakai screaming...the man laughing, his grip relentless...piranha swarming, tearing chunks from his pinkie...Malakai struggling...blood curling in the water like red smoke...

"Red Bellied Piranha have the strongest teeth of any piranha species," Malakai said. His flat voice made it clear that he was not really there in the motel room, but trapped back in time on one of the worst days of his childhood. "Eventually one of them just bit my finger off."

His severed pinkie, more bone than flesh, sinking to the bottom of the aquarium...the man releasing him... pulling his hand out of the tank...blood spurting from the stump of his finger ... Malakai running out the door, screaming for his father...

Sometimes it felt like he had never stopped screaming.

Malakai blinked several times, using the motion of his eyelids to scrub the memories from the forefront of his mind. His voice became normal again. "Ever since that day," he said, "I've been terrified of fish." He gestured toward the guppies Shiomi was holding. "So can we please get rid of those things now?"

Shiomi shook her head. "A badass gunslinger who's afraid of fish. File that one under 'Weird Shit I Never Thought I'd Hear'." She sounded amused, but not judgmental. Malakai had expected her to toss him a straight-jacket as she bolted out the door never to be seen again, so non-judgmental amusement was a response he could live with.

She slid off the bed and carried the bowl of guppies into the bathroom. He heard the sound of water splashing followed by the clank of the toilet handle as she flushed his demons down the drain. When she came back into the room, the bowl was empty. She set it on the dresser before sitting back down on the edge of the bed.

She leaned over and kissed him, letting her lips linger. "Thanks for telling me," she said softly. "I'm sure it's not an easy thing for you to talk about."

"I'd rather pour hot wax on my scrotum."

"I'll remember that for next time." Her smile was both naughty and surprisingly tender as she got up and began pulling on her clothes.

Malakai hated to see her gorgeous body covered up. He asked, "What are you doing?"

"I have to go."

"Why?"

"I have things to do."

"Things...or people?" He regretted it the instant it came out of his mouth. God, he was such a damn fool sometimes.

The hurt look that flickered across her face didn't make him feel any better.

"Shiomi, I'm sorry."

She tried to shrug it off, but he had clearly cut her deeper than she wanted to let on. "You're a bastard for saying it," she said as she walked to the door, "but you can make it up to me by taking me out for dinner tonight."

"Just tell this bastard when and where."

She opened the door. "Eight o'clock. The Atlantic Restaurant. Know where it is?"

He felt like a cold, hard fist had just punched him in the gut. "Yeah, but isn't that a—"

She grinned and closed the door, gone before he finished his question.

"—a sushi place?"

Malakai swallowed hard. He liked Shiomi, but he wasn't sure he liked her *that* much. Then again, sometimes you had to walk through hell to find an angel.

That angel has tainted wings, an inner voice cautioned.

Malakai did not ignore that voice. It spoke the truth. But throwing stones seemed unfair. Who was he to judge? Wasn't like his soul was whiter than virgin snow. He killed for a living—the paradoxical irony not lost on him—and had long ago given up any hope of finding heaven. But maybe, just maybe, it was enough to find someone with whom he could share his scars.

CHAPTER 10

MALAKAI SLEPT like the dead until mid-afternoon, then dragged himself out of bed and did the shower-shave thing. He moved gingerly to avoid tearing open his new stitches. The wound throbbed, but nothing he couldn't handle. Pain was an old, familiar friend and they knew how to deal with each other. He took the edge off with a handful of ibuprofen and a shot of the Jack Daniels that Shiomi had left behind. Not quite nectar of the gods, but good enough.

On the way to his standard end-of-the-day libation at Joe's, he stopped at a local bank and transferred all the nasty, incriminating photos of Senator Paula Olander from the briefcase to a safe deposit box he rented under an alias. He had safe deposit boxes—not to mention bus station lockers, subway lockers, etc.—scattered all over the nation as well as a few in Mexico, Canada, Australia, and Switzerland. Each rented with a different name, but all containing pretty much the same items: passports under various fake identities, $10,000 in emergency cash, and a Glock 17 9mm automatic with two spare magazines. The perfect gift box for a black ops bullet-slinger.

He didn't look at the photos as he added them to the stash. He had seen them once and once was enough. *More* than enough. His interest in the photos was practical, not salacious. He lived in a dirty world doing dirty business and sometimes the only way to not get buried under six feet of dirt was to have some dirt on important players. He didn't care how the senator got her jollies but he would be an idiot to pass up a Get Out of Hell Free card when it was dropped in his lap. He was many things, but an idiot wasn't one of them.

He arrived at Joe's earlier than usual and found the place deader than disco with only a pair of patrons nursing beers at a corner table. He ignored them as he told Joe all about Shiomi while a three-peat of Poison hits played on the jukebox, providing the story's soundtrack. The barkeeper stood there and listened in rapt attention, completely dumbfounded. So dumbfounded, in fact, that he apparently didn't even realize his usually-impeccable bow tie was askew.

"You're shittin' me," the bartender said.

"I shit you not," Malakai replied.

"No way." Joe shook his head. "Just no way."

"I'm serious, Joe, it really happened."

"Well, call me a monkey and spank my crank."

"Thanks for the offer, but I'll pass."

In the background, the jukebox switched to "Real Love" by Slaughter as Joe plucked two bottles of Red Dog out of the cooler, popped the caps, and plunked them down on the bar. "Have a drink on me and tell me all about it and don't forget I'm an old man, so I like to live vicariously. Give me all the juicy details."

Malakai grinned. "If you want to know how big my pecker is, just ask."

Joe snorted. "Nothing to talk about. All you white boys are hung like a field mouse. Besides, I don't give two craps about you. I want to hear all about her."

Malakai took a swig of beer and then said, "A gentleman never tells."

"Yeah, well, you ain't no gentleman and she sure ain't no lady, so I fail to see the problem."

Malakai put his beer down on the bar hard. Not quite a slam, but glass banged wood firmly enough to get Joe's attention. "Hey," Malakai said, "watch your mouth."

Joe paused with his own bottle halfway to his lips and stared at Malakai for a moment. "The fuck?" he said. Then his eyes popped wide open. "Oh, man, are you kidding me? Tell me you're kidding. Tell me you're not actually falling for this girl." He set the bottle down on the bar. "Holy shit! You are, aren't you." It wasn't a question.

Malakai shifted uncomfortably. "I didn't say that."

"Good God, Malakai, you could've walked in here and told me you'd found a leprechaun in your Lucky Charms this morning and I would've believed that before I'd believe you'd fall for a hooker." Joe shook his head. "For God's sake, Malakai, she's a whore! So she fucked you. Great! Wonderful! Hallelujah! But newsflash, sonny, that's what whores do. They fuck people. Don't go mistaking lust for love."

Malakai knew Joe was right. But he also knew Joe

was wrong. He also knew he would never be able to make his friend understand. He offered the only explanation he could. "She wasn't a whore when she was with me."

He finished his beer and slid off the stool.

"Where you going?" Joe asked.

"I have to meet a business associate." Malakai thought *business associate* sounded so much better than *ex-priest turned assassin handler*. "Then I'm meeting Shiomi at The Atlantis for dinner." Just saying the words made Malakai feel queasy. The fact that Shiomi had picked that restaurant proved she had a sadistic streak a mile long.

Joe reached up and scratched his grizzled cheek, then let his fingers trail along his chin thoughtfully. "You at a fish place, huh?" He seemed to ponder that miraculous turn of events for a moment, then observed, "You must really like this girl."

"I don't hate her, Joe, and for me, that's a pretty good start."

Joe leaned across the bar and slapped him on the shoulder. The wounded shoulder. Malakai winced slightly. He hadn't told Joe about catching a bullet. If the barkeeper caught the wince, he didn't let on. "Then I'm happy for you, man," Joe said. "I should probably apologize for some of the crap I just said, but I'm not going to." In a more serious tone, he added, "I just don't want to see you get hurt, that's all."

Malakai nodded. "I know. Thanks for the beer."

He left the bar, heading for his rendezvous with Father Thomas. Had he looked back, he might have seen Joe watching his departure with sad eyes and an even sadder smile, and perhaps he would have even heard his friend mutter, "Malakai, you sorry son of a bitch, that girl is gonna break your heart."

——————

When he arrived at the abandoned church a short time later, Malakai spotted Father Thomas' car. As usual, his handler had beaten him to the meet. Malakai didn't know why, but it was pretty obvious that the ex-priest liked to spend time alone in the church. Rays from the setting sun slotted down and shimmered off the stained glass windows as Malakai slipped inside, silent as a ghost. He didn't consciously avoid making noise; stealth was just part of who he was, as natural as breathing.

Father Thomas stood at the end of the aisle, gazing up at the crucifix and the crucified Christ impaled upon it, seemingly lost in trance-like thought and completely oblivious to Malakai's presence. Malakai walked down the aisle, still not making any noise, and though he could not see his handler's face, he sensed pain emanating from the ex-priest. Not random or generic, but a specific pain—the agony of something precious forever lost.

As Malakai edged closer, he heard Father Thomas say, ever so softly as he stared up at the cross, "Fuck You." The way he said it left no doubt that the "you" came with a capital "Y" attached to the front of it. Strangely, however, the obscenity was imbued with a hint of reverence as well. To Malakai's ears, it sounded like the "Fuck You" came from a deep, dark place where hate and love waged war with no clear victor emerging.

Or maybe he was just hearing things.

Malakai stopped right behind the ex-priest and said, "Sounds like you and God got some shit to work out."

Father Thomas nearly jumped out of his skin. He whirled around and glared at Malakai. "What is wrong with you, sneaking up on me like that? I could've killed you."

Malakai laughed. "*You* kill *me*? That's just crazy talk. You ever kill anyone?"

"None of your business."

"Yeah, that's what I thought." Malakai gestured at the crucifix. "Any particular reason you're dropping f-bombs on Jesus?"

Father Thomas shrugged. "Just pissed how my life turned out. I should be leading a flock, not juggling killers."

"If you don't like your life, change it," Malakai said, the same advice he had given Shiomi just this morning. "Go back to being a priest."

"I can't," Father Thomas said. "The Church won't let me." He hesitated, then added, "I did something a priest should never do. At the time it felt right, but now..." His voice trailed off.

"Now you're not so sure?" Malakai finished.

Another shrug from Father Thomas. "Sometimes I'm sure, sometimes I'm not. What I do know is this— what I did, I did out of love. If I had to live that part of my life over again, I'm not sure I would do anything different, right or wrong."

"What'd you do?"

"That's none of your damn business either."

"Sounds like you need therapy."

"Or a bullet in the head." When Malakai gave him a look, he hastily added, "Relax, I'm joking. I'm

Catholic, remember? For me, suicide is a one-way ride on a fast train to Hell."

"Maybe you think you deserve to burn for what you did back then," said Malakai.

Father Thomas' lips twisted into something resembling a smile, but with a grim, bitter edge. "I don't *think* I deserve to burn, I *know* I deserve to burn. But that's the beauty of the Lord's grace. What we deserve and what we actually get are two different things."

God, let's hope so, Malakai thought, probably the most honest prayer he had prayed in years. Aloud he said, "You're a scary guy sometimes, Tom."

The ex-priest snorted. "This coming from a guy who kills people for a living."

"You say that like it's a bad thing."

"It's not, when you do the job right." Father Thomas turned his head and glared at the assassin. "Speaking of which, what went wrong on the Abbott assignment?"

"Nothing. He's dead."

"We wanted those pictures retrieved, not destroyed."

"You said you wanted to prevent Senator Olander from being blackmailed by the Syndicate," Malakai retorted, "and that's been accomplished." He saw no reason to tell his handler that he had secreted away the photos for himself.

"I guess," Father Thomas said, but he was clearly unhappy. Changing the subject, he asked, "How's the shoulder?"

Malakai rotated his arm, testing the range of motion. He could feel Shiomi's stitches pulling, but they held. "I'll live," he said, "but scratch my name off the active duty list for week or two."

"When did you turn into such a candy-ass?"

Malakai ignored the jab. "And make sure that Orville guy gets a bonus or something, will you? He came through like a champ."

Father Thomas nodded. "Orville's one of the good guys. He knew me back in my priest days."

"Yeah, he told me."

Father Thomas stiffened, all of his muscles tensing at once, clearly alarmed. Maybe panicked would be a better word. In sharp, clipped tones he asked, "What exactly did he tell you?" He tried to sound nonchalant, but the nervous edge in his voice betrayed him.

Malakai had to admit that he was kind of amused to see his handler with the jitters. But he decided to let the ex-priest off the hook. "Relax, padre, he kept your precious secret. Just said he knew you back in the day."

Father Thomas exhaled, visibly relieved.

Judging from the ex-priest's reaction, Malakai figured the secret must be a whopper, but he had neither the time nor inclination to press further. As he turned to leave, he said, "I'll let you know when I'm ready to resume contracts."

"The bean counters will probably want a reduction on your fee for the Abbott job since you failed to retrieve the photos," Father Thomas said.

Malakai waved a hand dismissively. "Fine. Whatever."

"Really? You're not going to piss and moan and call us cheap bastards?"

"You are cheap bastards. But I'm not going to argue with you. Not tonight anyway."

"Where are you running off to in such a hurry?"

"I've got a date."

Father Thomas arched his eyebrows. "You? A date?" He shook his head in disbelief. "And they say the age of miracles has ended."

Malakai shot him the finger on the way out the door.

CHAPTER 11

AN HOUR LATER, Malakai found himself seated inside The Atlantis Restaurant, a sushi and seafood mecca for connoisseurs, a living hell for an ichthyophobe like himself.

Unsurprisingly, an aquatic theme dominated the décor, all soft blues and gentle greens. Paintings of marine life hung on the walls between outstretched fishing nets while model ships and boat anchors and buoys dangled from the ceiling on suspension wires that were nearly invisible in the soft, intimate lighting. A long bar of polished mahogany spanned the entire southern wall, a baleen whale carved into the wood in bas-relief.

It was all nicely done and aqua-chic, but similar décor could be found in plenty of restaurants in southern Florida. What made the Atlantis unique from other similarly-themed establishments were the tables, which consisted of actual aquariums. Patrons ate their meals as a variety of fish swam directly beneath them, separated only by a layer of glass.

In other words, it was an absolute nightmare for Malakai.

He sat at one of the tables, Shiomi across from him. She wore a yellow dress with a plunging neckline that exposed a brazen amount of cleavage, but Malakai barely noticed. He was too busy looking down at the fish swimming in fear-inducing proximity. He despised this weakness, hated the fact that he couldn't get it under control.

An assassin scared of fish? Seriously, what the hell is that?

But acknowledging the stupidity of his phobia didn't make it go away. Sweat dappled his forehead and it took every ounce of willpower to keep from trembling. He clenched his fists so tight that his nails dug into his palms and left crescent indentations.

"Malakai," Shiomi soothed, "relax, it's okay."

Some brightly-hued tropical fish about the size of a minnow floated by right beneath his salad fork. He didn't know what it was called, but it looked like a fish from that horror movie *Finding Nemo*. He couldn't control his shudder. "Why did you bring me here?" he asked. "Some kind of sick joke?"

"Believe it or not, I'm trying to help you."

"By giving me a coronary?"

"By forcing you to face your fear." Shiomi leaned forward. The movement gave him a great view down the front of her dress. He even managed to enjoy the sight for a fleeting second or two. Hell, maybe that was progress. "Obviously," she continued, "some part of your brain knows that these fish can't hurt you, but there's another part of your brain that is fixated on what happened to you when you were nine and that part takes over whenever you're around fish of any kind. So what we need to do is force the other part of your brain, the rational part, to take control. In other words, we want logic to dominate fear."

"You sound like a shrink."

She smiled. "I've known one or two in my time."

Malakai almost said, *I'll bet you have,* but managed to stop himself at the last second. Instead, he glanced over at a nearby table where a young couple clumsily used chopsticks to enjoy a plate of sushi. For a brief moment, he was sixteen again, puking up goldfish while still clutching the gun he used to kill his father. When the moment passed, he shuddered again and looked back at Shiomi. "Maybe *you* need a shrink," he said, "because you're crazy if you think I'm going to eat raw fish."

She batted her eyelashes and with exaggerated seduction asked, "What if I take you back to the motel, strip naked, and put the sushi all over my body?"

Malakai wasn't playing. "Then you'd be covered in dead fish and vomit," he said. "Not exactly how I envisioned this night ending."

"Oh really? And exactly how did you envision this night ending?"

"Naked Twister."

She laughed and despite everything, Malakai thought it was a beautiful sound.

The waitress appeared to take their order. Her black and white uniform looked crisp and clean, her voice cheerful as she greeted them. "Good evening and welcome to The Atlantis. Our specialty is sushi and we have the largest sushi menu in all of southern Florida. Could I start you off with some as an appetizer?"

"I'd rather eat a bullet," Malakai muttered, thinking about the .45 hidden under his sport coat. Maybe he should just pull it out and end his misery right now. Surely death couldn't be any worse than sitting at a table full of fish.

Shiomi smiled apologetically at the waitress. "Ignore him, he's in a bad mood. I think we'll just skip the sushi and go straight to entrees." She ran her finger down the menu and tapped on one of the selections. "I'd like the broiled salmon with a baked potato and Caesar salad on the side."

The waitress nodded. "Excellent choice." She turned to Malakai. "And for you, sir?"

Malakai studied the menu. "Got anything that doesn't have gills?"

The waitress smiled patiently. "Sorry, sir, we're a seafood restaurant." It could have sounded sarcastic, but it didn't; this girl was a true professional. "We do offer a surf and turf entrée, a petite filet mignon in butter sauce with a fillet of halibut."

"I'll have that, but hold the halibut."

"Malakai..." Shiomi scolded.

"Why get it if I'm not going to eat it?"

"Because."

"Really? Because? That's all you've got? Well, jeez, how can I argue with such devastating logic?" He looked at the waitress standing patient and silent throughout the exchange. "Bring me the halibut, just for the hell of it."

The waitress smiled again, collected their menus, and disappeared, no doubt heading into the kitchen to tell all the other servers about how it was just her luck to have to wait on the crazy guy. Hopefully she didn't spit on his fish. Then again, it wouldn't really matter, because he had no intention of eating the damn thing.

"Why did you make me order the halibut?" he asked.

Shiomi waved her hand. Her nail polish was dark red and freshly applied, evidence that she had actually taken time to pretty herself up for him. "No more fish talk," she said. "Let's talk about something else."

"Like what?"

"Tell me about your work. What's it like to do what you do for a living?"

"What do you want me to say to that?"

"The truth, of course."

"The truth." Malakai thought for a moment, then said, "Well, the money's good."

"Really?"

"Yeah, you make a killing," Malakai deadpanned.

Shiomi groaned. "Hopefully you're a better assassin than you are a comedian." She took a sip of her water, then said, "Seriously, tell me about your work. What was your first time like? What kind of gun do you use? Are you freelance or do you work for somebody? Any trouble sleeping at night? Do you aim for the head or do you go for the heart?"

"You really want to know all that?"

"Yes."

"Why?"

"Because that's what couples do. Get to know each other better."

Her word choice caught him off guard. "We're a couple now?"

Shiomi leaned forward, her eyes both intense and fragile. "We've slept together. We're having dinner together. Aren't those couple activities?"

"You sleep with a lot of men," said Malakai. "I'm sure some of them took you out to dinner before taking you to bed."

The words were out before he really thought about what he was saying and it was clear that they cut her, the hurt carved on her face like a razor slash. She hid it well, but she couldn't hide it all. It lingered for a sliver of a heartbeat, just long enough for him to catch it, and then she masked it with the seasoned practice of someone who was accustomed to being hurt and had long ago learned how to deal with it.

He silently cursed himself for being such a fool. He hadn't really meant to wound her like that. It was almost involuntary, his subconscious lashing out at the unfamiliar emotions she stirred within him. Almost as if the loneliness inside him felt threatened by Shiomi's presence in his life and rebelled against it.

But that didn't make it right.

He reached across the table and touched her wrist. "Sorry," he said. "I'm a jerk." Her skin felt warm beneath his fingers.

She waved away the apology. He noticed that she did it with her free hand, not the one he was touching. That one she left right where it was. "It's fine," she said. "Really."

He shook his head firmly. "No, it's not. Just because you're a..." His voice trailed off as his brain scrambled for a politically correct synonym for prostitute.

"Hooker?" she offered helpfully.

"That's not what I—"

She smiled. "It's okay, Malakai. I am what I am. No need to dance around the issue."

"Call yourself whatever you want," he said. "Still doesn't give me the right to be rude."

"Apology accepted. But we were talking about your job, not mine."

"Right." He leaned back in his chair and exhaled long and slow. "Okay, here goes," he said. "My first time was by far the hardest, because it was personal, not business. My gun of choice is a forty-five caliber auto. Most bang for the buck, in my opinion. Not too many targets stay vertical when they've been punched by a forty-five ACP. I'm technically a freelance operative, but most of my contracts come from one particular company."

Shiomi opened her mouth to say something.

Malakai cut her off. "Before you even ask...don't. If I told you, you'd probably be dead by dawn."

"Really? You're giving me the old 'if I told you I would have to kill you' cliché?"

"I wouldn't kill you," Malakai replied. "But someone else probably would."

"Well, isn't that comforting."

"As for your other questions," he continued, "no, I don't have any trouble sleeping."

"None at all? I find that hard to believe."

"Well, it helps that everybody I've killed needed killing."

"Even your first time?" Shiomi asked. "You said that one was personal. Did that person *need* to die or did you just *want* them to die?"

"Both," Malakai answered grimly.

Shiomi looked at him thoughtfully. Maybe she realized that he had just given her a glimpse, however brief, of the darkness within him. He met her gaze and did his best to lower his guard enough for her to see beyond his emotional defenses. He just prayed that she wouldn't run screaming when she saw the twisted tangle of hurt and scars and broken toys behind his eyes.

Then again, when he looked into her eyes, he saw the same thing.

It was a moment as intimate as their lovemaking, stretching hypnotically until the spell was broken by the waitress reappearing to refill their water glasses. "Your meals should be ready shortly," she told them. "Is there anything else I can get for you right now?"

"I think I'm ready for some wine," Shiomi said, reaching for the list propped up in the center of the table.

"I could go for a beer," said Malakai. "Any chance you carry Red Dog?"

The waitress shook her head with an apologetic smile. "I'm sorry, sir—"

They were the last words she ever spoke. Her voice —and her life—were suddenly silenced as bullets ripped into her from behind and her chest exploded outward in gaping blossoms of blood and bone. The high-velocity impacts punched her forward and she flopped facedown across the table. Alarmed fish flitted in every direction.

Malakai's combat skills kicked instantaneously into high gear. He burst into motion before the first drop of the waitress' blood even hit the floor. He threw himself sideways out of the chair and twisted his body toward where the shots had originated. Adrenalin rushed into his veins and fueled his survival instincts.

He quickly spotted the threat; two big, burly bastards wearing black leather jackets stood at the hostess station, sound-suppressed FN P90 submachine guns spewing brass in their hands. Not a very common assault weapon, but the bullpup design made it easy to conceal, which might have factored into the shooters' selection. He saw that the gunslingers were racially mismatched—one Hispanic, one Caucasian.

Malakai didn't know their names, but the Twins had come to town. And they were not playing nice.

He pulled Shiomi to the floor as bullets burned through The Atlantis. She looked terrified and covered her ears as a cacophony of violence hammered the place. Slugs shredded flesh and tore anguished screams from the dying. Glass shattered and furniture exploded into splinters. Chaos reigned supreme as Jesus and Joseph Twin ripped the restaurant apart with indiscriminate autofire. Innocent or guilty, they didn't give a damn as long as everyone died.

Malakai drew his .45, pulled Shiomi close, and shuffled them both behind the table. Being made of glass, it wouldn't offer much shelter, but it was better than nothing. "As soon as you get a chance, head for the bar!" He spoke loudly in order to be heard over the screams and violence.

Patrons made panicked dashes toward the exits, trampling each other in blind terror. Some made it out, but most were chased down by blazing streams of autofire and slaughtered well short of their goal. Bullet-riddled bodies twitched and jerked and spun and spurted and fell to the floor in spasming piles, one after another.

Malakai risked a glance around the edge of the table

and glimpsed the killers through the tendrils of gun smoke. The white guy appeared cool, calm, and down-right stoic, his face almost serene as he triggered steel-jacketed fusillades into helpless flesh. By contrast, his Hispanic companion had a crazy light smoldering in his eyes and a savage grin carved on his face as he unleashed hell from his stubby assault weapon.

Jesus' FN P90 chose that moment to run dry. Joseph's gun still chugged lead, but he was angled away from Malakai's position, his fire focused on a group of customers trying to flee out an emergency door. Jesus watched with a smirk as they all toppled like bowling pins, then ejected his spent magazine and reached for a fresh one with the practiced moves of a seasoned operator.

Malakai doubted they would get a better chance, so he seized the moment. "Now!" he said to Shiomi. "Go!"

They climbed to their feet and dashed for the bar. Over the chaotic din Malakai heard the Hispanic roar, "There's the *cabron*!" as he scrambled to insert another magazine.

Alerted by his partner's shout, Joseph swung around and sent a tracking line of fire toward the running couple. Jesus joined the fun a second later. The tables around Malakai and Shiomi exploded like ruptured balloons, hurling glass and water and fish in all directions. Malakai felt several fish bounce off him as he ran, which made him run even faster. In the midst of all the carnage, he didn't have time to ponder the absur-dity of being more afraid of getting struck by a fish than a bullet.

They dove behind the bar as high-velocity hornets ripped into the wood. Malakai felt a bullet just miss the back of his neck. Another plucked at his pants cuff. The twin 5.7x28mm salvos chopped into the mahogany and sent splinters flying everywhere like shrapnel. Malakai and Shiomi crouched down behind the bar as slugs hammered the shelves above them. Some liquor bottles shattered in liquid sprays; others fell to the floor as the shelving collapsed beneath them, eroded by relentless autofire. Malakai saw Shiomi wince as a large bottle of vodka bounced off her shoulder. No doubt that was going to leave a bruise.

If they didn't get killed first.

The two gunners raked the bar with their FN P90s, but the thick wood prevented the projectiles from penetrating. That was the good news. Bad news was, they were trapped back here.

Over the thudding impact of bullets, Shiomi said, "I never thought I would die in a seafood restaurant."

"I never thought I would *be* in a seafood restaurant," Malakai grumbled. "But we're not going to die. Not here, not now, anyway." He gripped the .45 tighter. The gun was locked and loaded, a round in the chamber just waiting for a target. "I need a distraction."

Slugs continued to pound their sanctuary as he looked around. He knew he didn't have much time. Eventually the autofire would chew away enough of the wood that the bullets would start popping through. If they were still stuck back here when that happened, some unlucky mortician would have a lot of fun plugging up all the holes in their corpses.

He grabbed the bottle of vodka that had fallen on Shiomi, a book of complimentary matches from a glass bowl stuffed behind the bar, and a cleaning rag. He noticed the screaming had lessened. Not a good sign. It meant most of the people in the restaurant were dead.

He stuffed the rag into the neck of the bottle and handed it to Shiomi. "When I light the rag, I want you to throw the bottle high in the air toward the far end of the bar. Got it?"

She took the bottle and asked, "What's your plan?"

"Kill these sons of bitches."

"I really like that plan."

Malakai could hear the FN P90s continuing to spit their sound-suppressed fire as he struck a match and touched it to the cloth. It caught instantly and the flame raced toward the bottleneck.

"Now!" he said.

Shiomi pulled her back arm, careful not to expose herself, and lobbed the bottle toward the end of the bar, arcing it up as high as she could. It was a good throw, exactly what Malakai had wanted. Though he couldn't see them, Malakai had no doubt that the Twins' eyes were naturally drawn to the sudden movement, automatically tracking the trajectory of the burning bottle.

Malakai snapped off a single shot that shattered the bottle in midair. The Molotov cocktail ignited in a whooshing explosion of orange flame.

Knowing he had the thinnest of openings, Malakai popped up from behind the bar like a gun-packing jack-in-the-box, the FNX-45 bucking in his hand. The two hostiles recovered from the fiery distraction quickly, but not quick enough. Not before Malakai punched a double-tap into the white guy's chest and ducked back down behind the bar. He didn't have time to stand there and watch the results, but he knew he had drilled both those bullets into Joseph's heart. Unless the killer was wearing Kevlar, he was dead on the floor just like all his victims.

His grim assumption was proven correct when he heard the Hispanic howl in grief-stricken rage. Renewed autofire raked the bar in long, sustained bursts as Jesus bellowed like a mad bull. "Malakai! You motherfucker! You killed my brother!"

Malakai was surprised the gunner knew his name, but he was even more surprised by the other revelation. He looked at Shiomi, puzzled. "Brother?"

"I'll explain later," she said.

Wait a minute. She can explain all this?

The thought did not make him happy.

Malakai pushed his unhappiness to a mental back burner as Jesus' submachine-gun continued to stutter and the giant Hispanic continued to shout threats that could best be described as colorfully obscene.

"You're fucking dead, Malakai! You hear me? Dead! I'm gonna eat your eyeballs and piss in the holes! I'm gonna cut off your *la polla* and shove it down your throat! You listening, *cabron*? You're gonna pay for this! By all that is un-fucking-holy, you're gonna pay!"

Crouched behind the bar, Shiomi looked at Malakai. "I think you made him mad."

"Yeah, I have that effect on people sometimes."

The gunfire suddenly stopped. Now all that was remained was the sounds of the wounded crying out in pain, the tortured wails of the grieving as they clutched the bullet-butchered corpses of their loved ones. Shiomi seemed distraught by all the anguished sobs, but Malakai simply shut them out. Fully engaged in survival mode, there was no time for sympathy. After a few moments, he cautiously peered over the top of the bar, ready to duck back down if it looked like he was about to catch a hot burst in the cranium. But there was no threat. The Hispanic giant had vanished, leaving his brother's fallen body behind. It lay in a pool of spreading crimson, sightless eyes staring up at the ceiling.

Malakai rose to his feet. "It's safe," he said. "He's gone." But he still kept his gun out.

Shiomi stood up as well. "After all that, he just leaves?"

A second later they heard sirens screaming in the distance, the pitch rising up and down in a familiar warbling pattern.

"That's why," Malakai said. "Cops are coming. We've gotta go."

Fire from the Molotov cocktail began to spread as they fled from the restaurant, smoke starting to billow up from the burning bar. The handful of survivors that had escaped the slaughter rushed toward the exit, fleeing the carnage. Malakai and Shiomi joined them. Shiomi looked horrified at the bloody bodies splayed everywhere, but Malakai barely gave them a second glance. Maybe he was callous or jaded or cynical or whatever label you wanted to hang on it, but he had seen this sort of thing more times than he cared to count. Life was violent and the innocent perished more often than the guilty. That's just the way it was.

Cold and cruel? Damn straight.

But that didn't make it any less true.

———

Once they were in the car and on the move, Malakai resisted the urge to stomp on the gas and peel rubber all the way home. Instead, he kept the Corvette just under the speed limit to avoid attracting attention. Several cop cars zipped past, heading toward The Atlantis, with lights and sirens blaring full blast. They were closely followed by two ambulances and a firetruck. Malakai shook his head. They were going to need more ambulances. And a coroner.

He glanced in his rearview mirror, watching the kaleidoscopic lights fade into the distance, and then returned his eyes to the road. "Okay," he said to Shiomi, "you said you could explain this shit, so who the hell were those guys?"

"Those were the Twins," she replied. There was a tremor in her voice and she looked a little frayed around the edges, but getting shot at will do that to you.

"Twins? They weren't even the same nationality."

"Twin is their last name," Shiomi explained. "Jesus and Joseph Twin."

"Really? A gunslinger named Jesus? You're kidding me."

"I swear to God." He couldn't tell if she was trying to be funny or not. "Joseph is the one you killed," she continued. "They're adopted brothers. They also happen to be assassins contracted with the Syndicate."

Malakai glanced at her in surprise. "How do you know about the Syndicate?"

"That's who I work for. I'm part of their prostitution ring in Miami."

Malakai felt like he had just been gut-kicked by a horse. All sorts of alarms shrieked in his head. "Shit," he muttered.

Shiomi asked, "What's wrong?"

He shook his head. He still couldn't believe what she had just said. "Damn it, Shiomi, the Syndicate put a bounty on my head." He punched the steering wheel in frustration. "How am I supposed to trust you when you work for the people who want me dead?"

"The Syndicate has a lot of people who work for them," she replied. "It's not like I'm part of the inner circle. You can trust me."

"No, I can't." He looked over at her, then returned his eyes to the road. "I can't trust you." Saying the words hurt more than he ever would have expected and the fact that they hurt at all told him that he had already let her get too close.

He wasn't the only one hurting, judging from the tone of Shiomi's voice when she quietly said, "If I wanted to kill you, I could have done it in bed this morning."

Malakai admitted it was a fair point, but it did little to put him at ease. "You're the one who arranged to have dinner at The Atlantis," he said. "For all I know, you set the whole thing up so the Twins could take me out."

"They were shooting at me too, remember?"

"Yeah, but they conveniently missed."

"They missed you too!"

Malakai didn't respond and they lapsed into silence for a few moments as another police car raced by, heading for the massacre they had narrowly escaped. A massacre carried out by a couple of killers that Shiomi seemed to know all about.

Ditch her, an inner voice advised. *Pull the car over,*

throw her out, and just drive away. Do it now before she gets you killed.

As if sensing his thoughts, Shiomi reached over and put a hand on his arm. Her touch was light, tentative, as if she feared he might lash out with a backhand. He would never do that—as far as he was concerned, only cowards and bullies hit women—but she couldn't know that. They might have shared a bed but they didn't really know each other, a fact that was sinking in with striking clarity.

"I didn't set you up," she said. "Believe me, if my father wants you dead, I'm the last person he would come to."

Wait...what? Malakai was puzzled. He was missing something. "What's your father got to do with this?" he asked.

"My father is Tanaka, head of the Syndicate's east coast operations."

"Well, of course he is." Malakai laughed bitterly. "Isn't that just great? My date happens to be the daughter of a crime lord who wants me in a coffin." He shook his head. "And they say God doesn't have a sense of humor."

Shiomi squeezed his arm. "You can trust me, Malakai."

She sounded sincere, but Malakai remained unconvinced. "Can I?" he said. "You're the daughter of the man who wants me dead."

Now it was Shiomi's turn to let out a bitter laugh. "Trust me, there's no love lost between me and my father. I hate him, Malakai. Hate him with all my heart and soul, with a hatred you can't even begin to fathom."

"Been my experience that love and hate are often the same thing."

"No, you don't understand," Shiomi said. "I *hate* him. He's the reason I became a prostitute."

"You became a prostitute just to piss off your father?"

"Not exactly." She took her hand off his arm and slumped back in the seat. "Take me back to the motel and I'll tell you everything."

CHAPTER 12

WHEN THEY GOT BACK to the motel, Malakai locked the Corvette and followed Shiomi into the room. She immediately grabbed the bottle of Jack Daniels and started slugging it down like a champion boozer. Whatever her story, Malakai doubted it was going to be butterflies and roses. You don't need whiskey to tell a fairytale.

Malakai sat down at the tiny table in the corner, took out his gun, and ejected the magazine. He said nothing as he topped off the mag, replacing the three rounds he had fired. No need to push her; she would tell him when she decided the time was right. He just hoped it was before she downed half the bottle.

He began field-stripping the .45 in order to clean it as she took a few more gulps. She swallowed hard, then carried the bottle over to the bed, propped up the pillows, and leaned back against the headboard. She let out a long sigh and then turned her head to look at him. "What do you know about the Syndicate?" she asked.

"They're a Japan-based criminal organization," he replied, "that evolved back in the nineties into an international entity with links to prostitution, narcotics, weapons, all sorts of bad business. They've also got their grubby little fingers into legitimate enterprises like oil and diamonds, all of which makes them extremely wealthy and extremely powerful. Rumor has it that even the Yakuza thinks twice before crossing swords with the Syndicate. Nearly every law enforcement agency in the world has taken a crack at them, with little success."

"That's because nobody talks in the Syndicate," Shiomi said. "Loyalty is law. It is both demanded and given. Those who have sworn allegiance to the Syndicate will kill themselves rather than be interrogated."

"Saw that firsthand myself," Malakai said, remembering the throat-cutting redhead in his apartment. "But if that's the case, why are you talking?"

"I work for the Syndicate," she replied, "but I'm not part of it, and I sure as hell don't owe them anything."

Malakai looked up from cleaning his gun. "I'm confused. I thought you said your father—"

She interrupted venomously. "My father is a goddamned bastard who gave me to the Syndicate when I was only twelve years old." The acid in her tone could have melted steel and she struggled to hold back tears.

Malakai was stunned. "Are you telling me...?" His voice trailed off in shock.

Shiomi stopped fighting the tears and let them drip down her face, tracks of pain gleaming like tainted diamonds on her high cheekbones. "I was twelve years old when I became a prostitute," she said quietly. "I was taken to a brothel in Tokyo where I was chained to a bed and gang-raped by a group of Syndicate soldiers to 'break me in'."

Malakai clenched his jaw so tight he nearly broke a couple of molars. He had never wanted to kill anyone more than he wanted to kill those nameless, faceless men who had done that to her. Not quick and easy deaths, either. No, he wanted to rip them apart with his bare hands. They deserved no less.

"A few days after that I began servicing clients and that's been my life ever since." Shiomi finished her story and took another pull from the bottle.

Malakai didn't know what to say. He had never heard such a horrible story. His own childhood had been hell, but nothing compared to what Shiomi suffered. "Why would your father do that to his own daughter?" he finally asked.

"Power," she replied. "Everyone who joins the Syndicate has to give them a gift, something of significant value, something that comes at a personal loss in order to prove your allegiance." She paused, took a deep breath, and then plunged ahead. "So my father gave them the most personal gift he could think of—me."

"What a son of a bitch."

"I don't think son of a bitch covers it," Shiomi said. "Anyway, when they made him head of east coast operations here in the States, they allowed him to bring me here so I could be close to him. But it doesn't matter, because I refuse to see the bastard."

Malakai quickly reassembled his pistol, inserted the fully-loaded magazine, racked a round into the chamber, and then set it down on the table before joining Shiomi on the bed. He didn't say anything at first; just pulled her close and wrapped his arms around her. She pressed into him as if trying to become one with him, perhaps subconsciously seeking the comfort and solace so brutally denied her as a child. She stifled any sobs but he could feel her tears soaking the front of his shirt. He didn't care; he just held her even tighter.

"God, Shiomi, I'm so sorry." He continued to hold her for several long minutes, both of them perfectly content to let the silence linger. She might be facing her own demons, but they weren't the only ghosts haunting the room. Listening to her tragic tale, his own violent past had been resurrected and clawed its way to the front of his mind. He finally broke the quiet by saying, "Your story reminds me of my own."

"How so?" She didn't move away, choosing to stay snuggled against him.

Malakai hesitated for just a fraction of a second. *Am I really going to tell her this?* But she had shared with him. Had opened up and shown him the scars on her soul. He owed her the same. "Because," he said, "you *wish* you could kill your father for what he did to you. I actually *did* kill mine. He was my first. I put two bullets in his head."

"Why?"

"Because he had it coming."

"That's not really an answer."

Actually, it was all the answer Malakai needed, but he knew he owed her more. "Okay, the story goes something like this." He took a deep breath and prepared to the face the demons that he usually kept banished to the back corners of his mind. "My father was a hardcore, diehard, born-again Bible thumper who would beat the hell out of me on a regular basis. Things got worse when my mother took off. Something in Dad's brain snapped and he became even more extreme, doing all kinds of crazy shit, including beating me with a big black Bible because he believed it was literally the rod of correction."

"Foolishness is bound in the heart of a child but the rod of correction shall drive it far from him," Shiomi quoted. "Proverbs twenty-two, verse fifteen."

Malakai was caught off-guard by the scripture recitation. "You know the Bible?"

"Just because I'm a whore doesn't mean I don't have faith."

"I'm surprised you have any faith left after what you've been through."

"Do you?" she asked.

It was a long time before he answered. "I don't know."

She seemed to ponder that for a moment before replying, "Well, I didn't say I have a whole lot of it. I'm just hoping a little is good enough."

Malakai hoped so too. For her sake, if not for his. "Anyway," he continued, "I think it's safe to say that my father was seriously fucked in the head."

Shiomi intertwined her fingers with his. Seeking solace for herself or for him, he wasn't sure. Nor did it matter. "Sounds like an understatement," she said.

"It gets worse," he said grimly. "Eventually Dad decided that in order for me to be more Christ-like, I needed to suffer just like Christ, so he made a cat o' nine tails and whipped me until my back bled."

"Oh my God!"

"About the only thing he didn't do was stick some nails through my hands and feet and hammer me to a cross, but he probably would have gotten around to that eventually." He paused. "But he ran out of time first."

"Because you killed him."

"Yeah."

Shiomi didn't say anything more, so Malakai continued. "Anyway, on my sixteenth birthday, Dad decides that my fear of fish is a sign of wickedness and needs to be purged, so he forced me to swallow the goldfish he kept in the living room."

Shiomi looked horrified. "Swallow them? You mean...alive?"

Malakai nodded. "I swallowed four of those fucking fish." He shuddered involuntarily. "I could feel them swimming around inside me as a I ran upstairs all freaked out, got my father's gun out of the nightstand, then came back down and put two bullets right between his eyes." He made a fake pistol with the thumb and index finger of his right hand and fired two imaginary shots. "Bang. Bang. Just like that."

Shiomi held his left hand a little tighter. "Have you ever regretted it?"

"No."

"Not even a little bit?"

"Never. My father was a bad man who deserved to die."

"Sounds like both our childhoods were royally fucked up."

"Not quite sure 'fucked up' does it justice."

She sat up and looked at him with her gorgeous almond-shaped eyes. "Maybe we're just two fucked up souls who were meant to find each other," she said softly.

Malakai held her gaze, happy to be lost in those dark pools, and felt something set his blood ablaze that could only be described as emotional recklessness. And for once, he didn't try to raise a shield or extinguish the flames; he just leaped into the fire. "Well, now that we've found each other, what are we going to do about it?"

"What do you mean?"

"Let's give this a shot, Shiomi. A real, honest to God, devil be damned shot."

"By 'this', you mean..."

"Us," Malakai confirmed. "I want to take a chance on us. Leave your old life, all the past, all the shit, leave it all behind."

She looked shocked and he couldn't blame her; he felt pretty shocked himself. He could hardly believe what he had just said. But he realized that he didn't want to take back his words. It might be reckless and crazy and foolish and completely contrary to his emotional composition, but he truly wanted to give this a try.

He watched intently as Shiomi wrestled with her own emotions. They played out across her face in rapid succession, a fast-moving pendulum of feelings that gave evidence of the conflict inside her.

He remained silent. There was nothing more to say. He had offered her his hand; it was her choice whether or not to take it.

She bit her lower lip. Not in a sensual, naughty-seductress way, but really chewing on it as she weighed his words. Finally she said, "I don't know, Malakai. It sounds nice, it really does, but there are severe consequences for turning your back on the Syndicate."

"The hell with the consequences." Malakai rasped the words with a fire that surprised even him. "We'll deal with them when the time comes. I'll bring this fight right to the heart of the Syndicate if that's what it takes."

Shiomi stared at him for several long moments, perhaps gauging the sincerity of his vow. He met her gaze and tried to communicate with his eyes just how serious he was. After what seemed like forever, she finally said, "If I do this, if I throw caution to the wind and put all my cards on the table, I need you to do something for me."

"Anything."

"Lay down your guns."

Malakai hesitated. That wasn't quite what he had in mind when he said "anything". He mulled it over, twisting it this way and that in his mind, exploring the angles. The most important question was, could he do it? Mothball the guns and give it all up?

It was less of a risk now than it had been just a few months ago. Before, assassins who walked away from the Company were often hunted down and exterminated by the nefarious Black Talon kill-squad. But then Gabriel Asher had gone toe-to-toe with Talon and destroyed them down to the last man, scorched earth all the way, no survivors. They learned the hard way that they should have just left him alone.

Rumor was the Company was rebuilding Black Talon, but it would take some time to bring the program back into play. Besides, Malakai knew he was more than good enough to tangle with professional exterminators and come out the other side the lone survivor. Not ego. Just fact.

It struck him that he now faced the same difficult decision Asher had faced a few months ago—whether or not to get out of the gun-for-hire game and start over, with a good woman by his side. Asher had walked away to be with Larissa. And the last time Malakai had checked in on them, still living at a fishing village in Mexico, Asher had made it clear he had no regrets and would do it all over again in a heartbeat.

So why the hell am I hesitating? Malakai wondered. What was there to even think about? He was asking Shiomi to give up her old life to forge a new one with him. She had every right to expect him to do the same.

Time to go all in.

"Deal," he said. "With one exception."

"What's the exception?" she asked.

"I'll kill to keep you safe. Anybody messes with us, I put a bullet in them."

Shiomi smiled. "I can live with that."

He took her face in his hands and looked deep into her eyes, trying to convey the gravity of their situation. He was running away from the Company. She was running away from one of the most powerful and unforgiving criminal organizations in the world. It was not going to be all sunshine and roses. In a serious tone he said, "This thing between us, whatever you want to call it, might very well get us killed."

Shiomi moved into his arms and kissed him long and hard. He pulled her close as he felt his passion start to rise, a passion Shiomi more than matched. She broke their kiss long enough to whisper, "Everyone dies, Malakai. Some just die happier than others."

And then there were no more words. Just the satin communion of flesh on flesh, heart to heart, soul to soul. Their desire burned hot and swift and when it was over, Shiomi lay beneath him, gasping and weeping, and whether from joy or fear, neither of them could say.

CHAPTER 13

TANAKA GAZED out his office window at the darkness. Clouds wisped in front of the moon, creating a contrasting interplay of light and shadow that danced upon the sand. He had been standing motionless in this position, hands clasped behind his back, for a long time, seeking tranquility in the rhythm of the nighttime shadows. Once, he had been able to achieve such tranquility quickly, almost on command, with nothing more than a proverbial snap of his fingers. Now that life had grown far more complicated, it took him much, much longer. Sometimes it never happened at all, making him wonder why he even bothered to try. But tonight he had finally managed to sink into a peaceful, Zen-like state.

It only lasted for a few moments before the door crashed open and Jesus stormed in.

Yoshi scrambled in behind him, as scraping and subservient as ever. "I'm very sorry, Tanaka-san, but he insisted on seeing you immediately and there was nothing I could do to stop him."

Tanaka doubted he had even tried. Yoshi possessed

many excellent, desirable skills as an assistant, but strong-arming was not one of them. Of course, possibly not even the gods of war could stop Jesus Twin when he was in a foul mood. Which was always.

As if to prove the point, Jesus hauled off and bitch-slapped Yoshi with a brutal backhand. The servant's lower lip split like an overripe strawberry as his head nearly popped off his neck. Had Jesus hit him any harder, he probably would have snapped a vertebra or two.

"Shut your fucking mouth," Jesus growled. "Your breath smells like shit from all that ass-licking and your yapping is getting on my goddamned nerves."

Tanaka sighed and turned away from the window. Tranquility would have to come later or perhaps not at all, and he could only blame himself. He was the one who had summoned this mad dog to Miami.

His face remained calm but expressed disapproval as he looked at the Hispanic hitman and said, "This is not how things are done in the Syndicate."

"Ask me if I care," Jesus retorted. "My brother is dead, killed by the bastard you sicced us on, and I want blood."

"Your wants are of no concern to me," Tanaka replied. "You were hired to do a job, you failed, and your incompetency resulted in your brother's death. That is a chance you take in your profession."

Jesus clenched his fists. "You pompous piece of shit, I'm gonna—"

"What you are going to do," Tanaka interrupted, "is get on a plane and return to Australia. The arrangements have already been made to get you out of town."

"The hell with that," Jesus snapped. "I'm not

getting out of town, *cabron*. What I *am* going to do is tear this town apart until I find Malakai." He stepped closer, using his height to tower over Tanaka, sneering down. "Now, you can either help me or you can tell me I'm on my own, but either way, the results will be the same: Malakai's head on a fucking pike." He paused a moment to smile evilly, then continued, "Difference is, if you point me in the right direction, things might be able to stay on the quiet side. But if I have to start knocking on doors on my own, I guarantee things are gonna get messy."

Neither the hitman's height nor his wicked grin impressed Tanaka. The *wakizashi* sword, resting in its wooden cradle on the corner of the desk, was within easy reach and Tanaka knew he could spill the arrogant assassin's greasy intestines all over his boots in the blink of an eye. For just the briefest of moments, Tanaka considered yielding to his baser instincts and doing just that.

But he resisted the urge and simply said, "Things are always messy where you are concerned." He regretted summoning the Twins to take out Malakai. He rarely made mistakes, but this had been one of them. Jesus and Joseph claimed to be the best of the best, but all they had done was publicly butcher a bunch of innocents and let their target escape. Hardly worth the small fortune he paid them. Not to mention the small fortune he paid the police detectives to deflect any heat away from the Syndicate.

"Don't call for a wrecking ball if you don't want shit wrecked," Jesus replied. "Now, what's it gonna be? I'm ready to ram some vengeance right up Malakai's ass. You know anyone who can point me in the right direction or should I start tearing this damn city apart?"

Tanaka normally did not respond well to threats. Capitulate to one threatening bastard and next thing you knew there were ten more bastards attempting to gain compliance through threats.

But he also knew that sometimes the path of least resistance was the wisest course of action, and now was such a time. Better to just give Jesus what he asked for and let him do his thing and be on his way.

"I believe there is someone who can help you," Tanaka said. "Someone who has helped us in the past." He looked at Yoshi, who was gingerly dabbing his bloody lip with a handkerchief. "Yoshi, give our Judas a call. If he asks for more money, remind him that we have already fattened his bank account quite nicely and yet somehow Malakai is still breathing."

Yoshi looked up, clutching the red-stained cloth. "You mean...?"

Tanaka nodded. "You know who I mean."

"He won't be happy, sir."

"He is merely a pawn and I do not concern myself with the happiness of pawns," said Tanaka. "If he is reluctant to cooperate, remind him that my sharks have not yet been fed tonight."

"Yes, Tanaka-san." Yoshi pulled a cell phone out of his pocket and began dialing.

Tanaka returned his gaze to Jesus. "Satisfied?"

Jesus grunted. "Not until I piss on Malakai's corpse."

CHAPTER 14

UNAWARE THAT A FEW miles away evil men plotted his demise, Malakai perched on his stool at Joe's and nursed a Red Dog while he told the bartender about his plans with Shiomi. He would never say it out loud—and Joe would rag on him mercilessly if he did—but it hurt more than he had expected to tell his friend he was packing up and moving on. There weren't too many things about Miami he would miss, but Joe was one of them.

For his part, Joe seemed surprised, but took it in stride. "You're really leaving town?"

Malakai nodded. "Shiomi's heading over to her place right now to pick up her things. Soon as I finish this beer, I'm gonna go break the bad news to her pimp."

"How do you think that conversation is gonna go?"

"That's up to him."

"Gotcha." Joe reached up and adjusted his bow tie. "Well, thanks for at least stopping by and letting me know you're getting the hell out of Dodge."

Malakai grinned. "Couldn't very well hit the road without saying goodbye, now could I?"

Joe looked at him sternly. "You're not gonna get all sappy and cry like a little girl, are you?"

"If there's a tear in my eye, it's not for you, it's for the great beer I'm gonna miss."

"Great beer? Yeah, right. Oughta be called Dog Piss."

"That's why I have to leave," said Malakai. "I don't need that kind of negativity in my life."

"Yeah, yeah, whatever." Joe gave his cleaning cloth a sharp, crisp snap and then flipped it over his shoulder. "What about your...uh...your job? You leaving that behind too or are you just gonna hang your shingle somewhere else?"

Malakai flicked a drop of condensation off his bottle as Cinderella began singing "Don't Know What You Got Till It's Gone" on the jukebox in the background. "I'm done with it all," he said. "New life. Starting over."

"You sound like one of those born again Jesus freaks."

"I don't know about born again. Maybe just looking for a little redemption."

"Well, you know what they say," said Joe. "Sometimes redemption is just one bullet away."

"Ain't that the truth."

The cordless phone behind the bar rang. Joe snatched it up and in a pleasant voice answered, "Joe's Bar and Grill." He paused for a moment and then all pleasantries vanished. "Are you kidding me? Now?" Another pause. "Yeah, I know I do a lot of business with you guys but that doesn't mean I have to drop everything just because you guys are incompetent." He paused one more time, listening to the voice on the other end of the line, and then growled, "Fine. I'll meet you out back."

He slammed the phone down.

"Problem?" Malakai asked.

Joe adjusted his bow tie, which had gone askew during his animated conversation. "Some delivery guy says he's out back with a load of Corona. Let me go take care of this and I'll be right back."

Malakai drained his bottle of Red Dog and set the empty down on the bar. "Don't worry about it," he said. "I have to bail anyway. Need to go have a conversation with this pimp, make sure he understands the nature of the situation and that coming after Shiomi would be hazardous to his health."

"Well, good luck with that," said Joe. "Good luck with everything, my friend."

"Thanks, Joe. Same to you."

The shook hands, firm but brisk, neither man the kind to drag out a goodbye longer than it needed to be. Their paths had crossed and they were both grateful for the years of friendship, but now their paths were diverging. Such was life and they both accepted it.

Malakai paused in the doorway on his way out to raise a hand in farewell. Joe returned the wave, offered him a smile tinged with sadness, then turned and headed out back. As Malakai stepped out into the night, he wondered if he would ever see the grizzled old bartender again.

———

As he made his way down the short, narrow corridor that led to the back storage room, Joe wondered if he would ever see his assassin—yeah, he suffered no delusions what that boy did for a living—friend again. Seemed pretty unlikely, since he and Shiomi were about to piss off some pretty nasty people, which meant they could never set foot in Miami again.

Malakai, you reckless son of a bitch, I hope it all works out for you.

As he stepped into the storage room, Joe found himself face to face—well, face to chest, actually—with a giant Hispanic that he had never seen before.

"You Joe?" the giant asked gruffly.

"The one and only. I take it you're the delivery guy?"

The man nodded. "I'm Jesus."

"Let me guess—last name Christ?" Joe shook his head. "Let's see what you got for me."

He never saw it coming. Jesus' fist moved in a short, vicious snap that connected with Joe's face. One second he was upright, the next second he hit the floor with a thud.

Just before unconsciousness claimed him, the bartender heard Jesus say, "A whole lot of pain, amigo. That's what I've got for you. A whole lot of pain."

And then the world went black.

————

When the lights came back on in his brain, Joe found himself naked and hanging from chains wrapped around his wrists and tossed over a large hook embedded in the ceiling, pulling his arms over his head so that they were nearly wrenched from their sockets. He could just barely touch the floor with the tips of his toes. He started to tell himself that he had been in worse predicaments, but then stopped. Who was he kidding? He was in some serious shit here.

He managed to get enough traction with his toes to twist around until he saw an arched doorway. Near as he could tell, he was chained up in a small alcove off another, much larger room. He saw water, some sort of giant pool with colored lights reflecting off the surface. At first he thought it might be a swimming pool, but he couldn't smell any chlorine. In fact, it smelled more like the ocean, with a saltwater tang in the air.

He did a double-take as a dorsal fin sliced across his field of vision. "What the...?" he muttered to himself.

He shook his head and blinked rapidly several times and when he looked again, the dorsal fin had disappeared. Probably a delusion brought on from being coldcocked.

He surveyed the room, his prison, taking in the white ceramic tiles, the concrete floor, and the large drain right between his feet. It did not escape his notice that the concrete around the drain was stained a reddish color. If he was lucky, it was just rust. But he wasn't feeling particularly lucky right now. And the large chainsaw and portable blowtorch on the stainless steel table in the far corner of the room did not exactly make him think that life was about to become all rainbows and unicorns.

Joe swallowed hard and muttered, "I don't think this is the Holiday Inn."

If the chains, dorsal fin, blood stains, and chainsaw hadn't already put ice in his bowels, the sight of two men—Jesus and Tanaka, though he only recognized Jesus—entering the room wearing black raincoats and safety goggles would have.

At that exact moment, Joe abandoned all hope of survival and silently prayed that he died like a man. He had lived a good life, but it looked like the end was going to be one rough ride.

Jesus carried a big bucket over and set it down by Joe's feet. The raincoat rustled loudly when he walked, usually an innocent enough sound but quite disturbing in this context. The grin he gave Joe would have looked right at home on the face of the devil himself. "For the pieces," he said cheerfully.

Joe refused to show them any fear. Looked like his life was about to come to a violent end, but that didn't mean he had to go out like a bitch. "You bring a big enough bucket?" he asked. "I'm just a little ol' black man, for God's sake. I won't fill that thing up even halfway."

Jesus' grin broadened. "You've got *mucho cojones*, amigo. Maybe those will be the first thing I cut off." He walked over and patted the chainsaw with mock affection as he leered at Joe.

Tanaka joined the conversation. "Perhaps we are getting ahead of ourselves," he said. "Perhaps there will be no need for any cutting at all." He glanced at Jesus. "*Cojones* or otherwise."

Jesus looked disappointed by such a thought.

"Perhaps," Tanaka continued, "our friendly neighborhood bartender will simply tell us what we want to know and spare himself more pain than he could ever imagine." He smiled at Joe, a shark's smile, cold and merciless. "How about it, Joe? Is there any chance you will cooperate without things getting, how shall we say...messy?"

Joe listened to the smooth, clipped, oily tone of the man's voice and instantly disliked him. Of course, that might also have something to do with the fact that the man was threatening to chop him up with a chainsaw. As first impressions went, that made a lousy one.

"Depends on what you mean by 'cooperate'," he said. "If by 'cooperate' you mean get down on my knees and give you a hummer, then the answer is not only no, but hell no. But if by 'cooperate' you mean run down to the Seven-Eleven and get you a grape Slurpee, then sure, just take these chains off and I'll be back in a jiffy."

Tanaka's smile vanished. "Tell us where we can find Malakai," he said in a commanding voice that sounded like it was accustomed to being obeyed.

"That's easy," said Joe. "In the Bible, right between Zechariah and Matthew."

Jesus chuckled. "Man, you are one stupid fucker."

"And you've got a dirty mouth," Joe retorted. "You dick-smoking, pig-licking piece of no-good shit."

Jesus' lips curled into an evil smile. "Old man, it is going to be my supreme pleasure to mess you up, it really is." He walked over to the table, picked up a file, and began sharpening the teeth of the chainsaw. The rasp of metal on metal sounded unpleasant in the close confines of the alcove.

Tanaka seemed immune to the noise. Still standing in front of Joe, he said, "No more games. Tell us where Malakai is. We have it from a very reliable source that you and he are friends, that he frequents your bar."

"I have no idea where he is," Joe replied. "He comes in, has a beer, a little chit-chat, he leaves. That's where our relationship, if that's what you want to call it, begins and ends. If you want to find Malakai, you've got the wrong guy."

"What if I told you that I do not believe you?"

"Then I'd tell you that just because you don't believe something doesn't mean it ain't true. After that, I'd probably tell you to pucker up and kiss my black ass."

Tanaka's cold eyes bored into Joe with the intensity of a cobra's stare. "Perhaps after a period of persuasion you will be a bit more forthcoming with the information we require."

He stepped back and motioned to Jesus.

The burly killer picked up the chainsaw and walked over to where Joe hung in chains. "Feel free to scream," he said. "That's kind of the point."

Pain. Torture. Agony. Joe knew it was all about to be delivered in spades. He steeled himself for the hell to come as Jesus yanked the starting cord and the chainsaw rumbled to life. He revved the throttle a few times, making the motor roar, then gave Joe a wicked grin. "Now, where should we begin?"

Joe soon found out the answer to that question.

Start at the bottom and work your way up.

CHAPTER 15

SHIOMI'S PIMP lived in a studio apartment by himself. Which was for the best, given his rather peculiar sexual proclivities. You could call him perverted or you could call him adventurous, but you certainly could not call him normal. He kept the apartment decorated like a '70's love-nest, complete with a disco ball roughly the size of the Goodyear blimp, a lava lamp, and a heart-shaped water bed with satin sheets.

On the bed sprawled what appeared to be a naked man wearing nothing but knee-high black leather biker boots, but in actuality was a full-size synthetic love doll that bore more than a passing resémblance to the lead singer for Judas Priest. Anatomically correct, the doll's prick perched in a permanent plastic erection that would make John Holmes blue with envy.

The pimp was a pasty-white scarecrow of a man wearing purple bikini briefs, white bunny slippers, and a green feather boa as he danced around the bed with maniacal energy like an albino monkey jacked up on crystal meth. As he whirled and twirled and pirouetted, the pimp snapped photos of the love doll with a digital camera, crooning in a soft, silky, effeminate voice.

"Oh, yeah, big boy, that's good. Better than good. Purrrrrrrrrfect." He trilled the r's into the sound of a cat purring and then giggled like a little girl. "Don't you move a muscle, handsome." Another naughty giggle. "Well, unless it's your love muscle."

The camera went *click-flash* as he snapped another picture.

"Oh, baby, you are soooooo hot." The pimp growled sultrily. "I could eat you for breakfast, lunch, and dinner, and still have room left for dessert." He grinned coyly at the doll. "And you know what I like for dessert, don't you, big boy."

He raised the camera again.

Click-flash.

"Oh, big daddy, the things I'm gonna do to you. You an' me, we're gonna make sweeeeeeeet rock 'n' roll together. You betcha, baby. You rock my world and I'll rock yours."

Click-flash.

This time a *thud-thud-thud* followed the *click-flash* as someone knocked on the door.

The pimp nearly jumped out of his alabaster skin. He turned toward the door with a frown. The knock sounded firm, more banging fist than rapping knuckles, not the tentative tapping of a Jehovah's Witness trying to tell him about the Kingdom or a Girl Scout trying to fatten him up with Thin Mints. Not that either of those groups frequented this part of town.

"Who is it?" he called out, giving the feather boa a flick.

"Just open the door," said a man's voice. "It's about Shiomi."

The pimp pranced over to the door and peered through the peephole. He didn't recognize the face on the other side and the face looked decidedly unfriendly. Certainly not the kind of face that made him want to open the door.

He stepped back. "I don't know you and I have a firm policy about not opening my door for people I don't know," he said. "Now what's this about Shiomi? You know where she is? Because that bitch has got some serious explaining to do. Busted a customer's nose two nights ago and hasn't been heard from since." He stepped back up to the door. "Nobody can find the stupid whore." He put his eye up to the peephole again...

...just in time to see the stranger raise his foot to deliver a kick. The pimp jumped back with a girlish yelp as the door smashed open and a very pissed off Malakai stormed into the apartment.

"The next time you call Shiomi a stupid whore," Malakai rasped, "I'm going to put a dozen hollow-points in your goddamn guts, got it?"

"Ohhhhhhh," the pimp crooned mockingly, "you're a big bad tough guy, aren't you? You gonna rough me up, slap me around? I like that in a man." He raised the camera. "Smile pretty, big boy."

Click-flash.

Malakai slapped the camera out of his hand. It hit the floor but didn't break, skidding up against the wall. The pimp retreated, slinking backward until his legs hit the bed. He sat down, making the water inside the mattress slosh as Malakai followed him across the apartment, as relentless as a mongoose hunting a snake.

"Do you know who I work for?" the pimp whined.

"Yeah," said Malakai. "I do. Ask me if I care."

"If you so much as lay your little pinkie finger on me, I can make your life miserable with just one phone call."

"You aren't gonna do anything except shut your mouth and listen to what I came here to say to—" Malakai abruptly stopped talking as he saw what was laying on the bed. "What the hell kind of sick shit is this?" he growled.

"Who you calling sick?" The pimp seemed genuinely offended. He turned his head and gazed adoringly at his synthetic companion. No man had ever looked on a woman—or another man—with such deep, devoted affection. He turned back to Malakai and said, "What I do in the privacy of my own home is my business. If you recall recent events, I didn't invite you in here." He raked his gaze over Malakai's firm, fit frame and smiled. "Though I probably would have, if you had promised to play nice. Know what I mean?" He followed the smile up with a lascivious wink and waggled a bunny slipper-clad foot at Malakai.

Malakai whipped out his sound suppressed FNX-45 and shoved it in the pimp's face. "Are you trying to get shot?"

The pimp's smile wilted. "Now, see? That's not playing nice." He pretended to pout, even giving his lower lip a quiver.

"Shut your mouth and open your ears," Malakai rasped, "because I'm only saying this once."

The pimp made a zipping motion across his pouting lips.

"Shiomi is done," Malakai said. "She's leaving the business, coming with me. She's not yours anymore. You're going to let her go, no questions asked, and don't even think about trying to get her back."

"Yeah? Or what?"

Malakai shifted the gun's aim and fired a single shot that exploded the love doll's oversized erection like a pin-pricked balloon.

"Or I'll do that to you," he said. "Any questions?"

Tears streamed down the pimp's face as he stared sadly at his castrated playmate and shook his head. "You bastard," he moaned. "You heartless, heartless bastard."

"Yeah, I'm a real son of a bitch. You might want to keep that in mind before you think about coming after us."

The pimp started collecting pieces of the rupture love doll. "The Syndicate won't let her go."

"You just take care of your boyfriend there," Malakai said. "I'll take care of the Syndicate."

Message delivered, he exited the apartment. He had better things to do with his time than waste it on this twisted creep. He probably should have just popped a hollow-point into the pimp's snot-locker and been done with it. Would have been a whole lot faster.

As soon as he was gone, the pimp picked his digital camera up off the floor, pranced over to his computer, connected the camera to the machine, and downloaded the last photo. Malakai's hard, grim face filled the screen. He picked up his phone and dialed a number he was never supposed to call unless it was an absolute emergency. He was guessing this qualified.

As the phone rang, the pimp glared at Malakai's image and muttered, "Okay, Mr. Tough Guy, I'll show you who you're messing with."

CHAPTER 16

IN THE POOL room of Tanaka's beachside mansion, the tiny alcove had become an abattoir. Blood and screams soaked the walls, with more of both yet to come.

Joe dangled from his chains, seized by pain beyond description, his legs amputated at the knees by the chainsaw. Head slumped on his chest, through an agonized fog, he could see his blood spurting copiously, life rushing from severed veins and arteries. Somewhere in the back of his dazed mind, he wished for it to spurt faster. Blood loss would lead to death and that was all he could hope for at this point.

He avoided looking at the bucket. He had made the mistake of doing so just once and the sight of his chopped-off legs sticking up out of the pail like grisly props for some grade-B horror movie would haunt him until he died. Which, hopefully, would not be long now. He didn't pray to God; he prayed to the Reaper, and begged him to come quickly.

Jesus turned off the splattered chainsaw and eyed

the gushing blood. He turned to Tanaka, who stood in the corner, watching with hooded eyes. "Stupid *bastardo* is trying to bleed to death on me." His eyes swung back to Joe. "Hey, Joey boy, this is unacceptable, trying to check out of the game before the game gets good. This—" he waved at the amputated limbs "—was just a warm up, amigo. Nothing but foreplay. I haven't even begun to fuck you up yet. So let's see what we can do about all that bleeding."

He swapped the chainsaw for the blowtorch and applied the 3,600 degree flame to the butchered stumps of his victim's legs. Joe thought he had known pain before, but this was worse—much worse. Hell had come to earth and he was trapped in the inferno. It was more than he could bear. He opened his mouth as wide as it would go and screamed as the fire cauterized his flesh and tissue. But even his howls of agony could not drown out the sizzling noise that filled the room. It sounded like bacon grease on a hot griddle.

Jesus kept the flame steady until he had turned the stumps into a charred mess and stopped the bleeding. He turned off the torch and studied his gruesome hand-iwork. Nodding in satisfaction, he walked back over to the table and retrieved the chainsaw, then gave Joe a toothy grin. "Now, where were we?"

Joe steeled himself for more pain, but before Jesus could get back to work, Yoshi rushed into the room with a piece of paper in his hand and hurriedly approached Tanaka. "I am very sorry to disturb you, Tanaka-san, but I just received a phone call from Shiomi's pimp."

"He has been instructed not to use that number unless it is an emergency. I trust he had an acceptable reason for calling?"

Yoshi nodded. "He was visited by a man who said that he and Shiomi were together now and she was leaving the Syndicate."

Tanaka's only reaction was to raise his eyebrows ever so slightly. "I see. Did this mystery man give his name?"

"No, but the pimp managed to take his picture. He emailed it to me." Yoshi handed the photo to Tanaka. He looked very pleased with himself, like a dog that just fetched a ball and now awaits a pat on the head from the master.

As Tanaka studied the picture, Jesus wandered over for a look. His eyes bulged big and angry. He tapped his finger against the photo, hard and vicious. "That's him! That's Malakai! That's the *bastardo* who killed my brother!"

Tanaka folded the photo in half and ran his finger along the crease as he pondered this turn of events. It only took him a few moments to reach a decision. He gestured at Joe. "We no longer need him. Put him out of his misery." He handed the photo back to Yoshi. "Have Shiomi picked up and brought to me."

"What's your plan?" Jesus asked.

Tanaka's lips twitched in a soft smile. "Why hunt a rat when you can make the rat come to you?"

"As long as I'm the one who gets to kill the rat, it's fine with me."

"I do not recall asking for your approval." Tanaka waved a hand toward Joe again. "Finish him, please. It is almost time to feed the sharks."

Jesus revved up the chainsaw again and raised it toward the bartender's neck. The last thing Joe saw before he died was Jesus' wicked grin. And then there was nothing but crimson death as the blade ripped into his throat.

———

Shiomi glanced around her apartment one final time, trying to shake the unexpected melancholy. Yes, it was just an apartment, nothing special about it, but it had been her home for many years. She was surprised to realize she would miss it. But she certainly would not miss the life she had been forced to live while residing in the apartment. This place might have been home but her life had been hell and now she had a shot at a fresh start with a man who was every bit as soul-scarred as she was. If that meant leaving the comforting familiarity of her old apartment, then so be it.

She packed everything she cared to bring into a duffel bag which she hoisted over her shoulder. It weighed almost nothing, proving there was little in her life that she cared about, which made it that much easier to say goodbye and start over. She killed the lights, gave the apartment one last glance to seal in the memories she wished to keep, and then turned to leave.

When she opened the door, three Syndicate soldiers stood there. They didn't waste time with pleasantries. One of them said gruffly, "Your father wants to see you."

She sighed in annoyance. "The feeling isn't mutual."

"You don't have a choice."

"Yeah," Shiomi said. "Story of my life." She stepped out into the hallway and was escorted away by the three men.

While waiting for Shiomi to arrive, Tanaka poured himself a scotch on the rocks and watched a news report of Senator Paula Olander speaking to the press and vowing to exhaust all available options to hunt down "the heartless bastard" that had murdered her husband and bring them to justice.

As he sipped his drink, Tanaka smiled thinly. *Fear not, Senator, the heartless bastard will be dead soon. Except, he is not heartless. In fact, his heart is exactly what will get him killed.*

He had not abandoned his plans to sink his hooks into the senator. But with both her husband and nephew dead and the salacious photos destroyed, he would have to seek alternative options to snag Senator Olander in the Syndicate's powerful web. Maybe they could somehow frame her for Malakai's imminent death—make it look like she had contracted a hit—and then blackmail her into cooperating with them. He took another sip of scotch and mulled over the idea. It definitely merited further contemplation.

Someone knocked on his office door. A tentative knock that made Tanaka frown. He set his drink down on the desk and said, "Come in."

Yoshi entered, looking extremely uncomfortable, and closed the door behind him. He nervously wrung his hands and shuffled his feet, but said nothing. He seemed unable to meet his master's eyes. Not a good sign.

"What is it, Yoshi?" Tanaka roughened his voice enough to let his servant know that he expected answers, not downcast glances and foot-shuffling. "Where is Shiomi?"

Yoshi straightened his posture and stopped wringing his hands. He met Tanaka's stare and replied, "Just outside, sir."

"Then bring her in."

Yoshi hesitated for a fraction of a heartbeat, then said, "I must warn you, sir, she is in handcuffs."

"What?" Tanaka practically bellowed the word. "Why? She is my daughter and should have been treated as such."

Yoshi looked like he wanted to be anywhere but here, perhaps fearing that the master would punish the messenger because the message displeased him. "She attacked one of the men," he said. "Scratched his face very badly. It is very likely that he will lose his left eye."

"Did he deserve it?"

"I do not know the details, sir."

"I see." Tanaka was confident he knew the details without even asking. But he would ask anyway. And then he would dole out punishment. "Bring her in."

Yoshi opened the door and three Syndicate soldiers hauled Shiomi into the room, hands cuffed behind her back. Even shackled, Tanaka thought she looked fierce, indomitable. Despite what he had been forced to put her through in order to achieve his goals, she was still his daughter, and he took pride in her unbroken spirit.

Evidence of that unbroken spirit was clearly etched on the face of the man to her left, who suffered from four deep scratches gouged diagonally across his features, as if he had been swiped by a tiger's paw. Pale fluid oozed from his damaged eye, tracking down his cheek like a tear.

"Remove those handcuffs at once," Tanaka snapped, making his irritation clear to everyone in the room.

The soldier on Shiomi's right hastened to obey. Once the metal bracelets were off, Shiomi rubbed her chafed wrists and glared at her father. "Dad," she said, sneering the word into a sarcastic obscenity. There could not have been less endearment in her voice if she tried.

Her hatred slashed at him, as it always did. But he refused to show any sign of hurt, as he always did. He ignored her rebellious tone and said, "Explain to me what happened."

"Simple. One of your goons wanted to play grab-ass, so I ripped his face off for him."

Tanaka's eyes shifted to the wounded soldier. "You had the audacity to touch my daughter?"

The man looked like a crippled lamb facing a wolf. "Tanaka-san...sir...I just...she's a... well, you know..."

"She's a what?" Tanaka demanded coldly. "Go on, say it."

"I'd rather not, sir."

"Say it!"

The soldier looked miserable and pathetic, a man without hope, without options. "She's a whore, sir."

"That is correct, she is a whore. But she is also more than that—she is my daughter. And as such, you had no right to lay your hands on her in that manner." Tanaka gestured toward the soldier's face. "Does your eye hurt?"

The man nodded. "Yes, Tanaka-san."

"Let us see if we can rectify that. I despise seeing any of my men suffer needlessly. Take out your gun."

Slowly, the soldier pulled out his Glock 23.

"Very good," said Tanaka. "Now place the barrel against your eye and pull the trigger and all your suffering will cease." He kept his voice deceptively calm and neutral, as if he had told the man to take two aspirin and call him in the morning instead of ordering him to put a bullet through his orbital socket.

The soldier just stared at Tanaka in disbelief.

Accustomed to immediate obedience, the man's hesitation infuriated Tanaka. The lines of his face hardened and his lips tightened into a merciless slash. "I can have twenty men at your house in less than ten minutes," he warned. "I will have your family cut into pieces and fed to the sharks like chum. Is that what you want?"

The man hurriedly shook his head. "No, Tanaka-san."

"Then obey me."

No more hesitation. The soldier raised the gun, put the muzzle against his wounded eye, and pulled the trigger. The .40 caliber bullet blasted a sizeable portion of his brains out the back of his skull. His lifeless corpse hit the blood-splashed floor.

Tanaka gestured at the remaining two soldiers. "Remove him from my sight."

The soldiers each grabbed one of the dead man's arms and dragged the body from the room, leaving behind a wet slick of gore-matted hair and shattered bone fragments. Yoshi followed them out, careful not to step in the mess, and closed the door behind him.

Alone at last with his daughter, Tanaka turned to Shiomi. "I am sorry you had to witness that, but I am even sorrier for what he did to you."

"You must have a real god complex going on in that head of yours, you know that?" Shiomi looked disgusted. "Some guy cops a feel and you have him killed."

"He died because he treated you like a whore."

"He may have treated me a whore, but you *made* me one, Dad." Again, she sneered the endearment into something ugly, like a rose covered in muck and crushed underfoot. "Why did you bring me here anyway? You know I don't want anything to do with you."

Tanaka sighed heavily. "Why must you hate me so? I just killed a man for you. Doesn't that mean something?"

"Sure it means something. It means you know a lot about power but not a lot about love."

Tanaka captured her eyes and held them, willing her to see the sincerity in his gaze. "Listen to me, Shiomi, and listen well. I am not a good father. I know that. I have failed you beyond measure."

"Understatement of the year," she scoffed.

"But I do love you," Tanaka continued. "You may not believe it, but I do. More than you can ever know."

"You're right," Shiomi said. "I don't believe you. But if you want to prove it to me, let me go."

"I can't do that. Not yet."

"Why not?"

"Because I need you to tell me about Malakai."

Shiomi stared at him blankly, the perfect poker face. "Who?" But her heart betrayed her, beginning to pound loudly in her chest.

"We are past the time for games," said Tanaka. "I know that you and Malakai are planning on running off together, trading your old lives for a new life together. Do you love this man, this... murderer?"

Shiomi laughed mockingly. "*You're* calling *him* a murderer? That's precious. And yes, I do love him. I never thought I could love someone after what you did to me, but I do."

Tanaka could not believe what he was hearing. "You are my daughter and a daughter of the Syndicate. It is completely unacceptable for you to love one of our enemies."

"Sorry," Shiomi said, though she didn't sound sorry at all. "But you can't control love. It doesn't work that way. It isn't something you can tame or lock away in a box or put a leash on."

"Of course you can," Tanaka countered. "The ability to master my emotions has made me the man I am."

"Having no emotions doesn't make you a man," Shiomi said. "It makes you a monster."

Regret filled Tanaka's heart as he realized he could not reason with his daughter. "You truly hate me, don't you?" he asked softly. It wasn't really a question.

Shiomi injected all the venom she could muster into her words as she replied, "With every inch of my heart and soul."

Tanaka stared at her thoughtfully for several long moments, then reached a decision. His features abruptly hardened and when he spoke, his voice was cold, flat, ruthless, and utterly devoid of emotion. "If that is how you feel, then so be it. If it is hate you desire, then hate you shall have. From this point forth, you are no longer my daughter. Now you are just bait."

"What do you mean, 'bait'?"

Tanaka ignored her question and pressed a button his desk. Seconds later, the office door opened and the two soldiers stepped back inside. The one on the left said, "You summoned us, Tanaka-san?"

"I did," Tanaka replied. "Have the remains of the bartender been removed from the alcove?"

The soldier nodded.

"Good." Tanaka pointed at his daughter. "Put her in there for the night. Let her hang from the chains and ponder what is going to happen to her beloved Malakai when he comes for her."

As the soldiers stepped forward and gripped her arms, Shiomi looked at her father and said, "When he gets here, he's going to kill you."

Tanaka picked up his glass and gave her a shark-like smile. "We shall see."

He sipped scotch as his soldiers dragged her out of sight.

CHAPTER 17

WHEN MALAKAI RETURNED to his motel room and turned on the lights, he was surprised to find that Shiomi wasn't there yet. She was supposed to go to her apartment and pack a bag while he said goodbye to Joe and dealt with her pimp, then meet him back here.

He shook his head. How long could it take to grab a few things? Then again, he'd been a bachelor all his life, so he didn't have a clue about women's packing procedures.

He shrugged off his jacket, draped it over the back of a chair, and kicked off his boots. He set his .45 on the nightstand before turning off the lights and stretching out on the bed. The sheets still smelled of Shiomi's perfume, a subtle scent with exotic hints.

He glanced at the red LED numbers on the alarm clock—11:22 p.m. Where the hell was she?

He settled back against the pillows and shut his eyes, planning on just power-napping until Shiomi showed up. But apparently his body decided it need more than some quick shut-eye, because when he awoke, the clock glowed 2:13 a.m.

"Shit!" He sat up in bed and peered around the dark room. He couldn't believe he had slept that long. In his line of work, if you slept like the dead, you ran the risk of ending up actually dead. "Shiomi, you here?"

Silence.

Well, not really silence; he could hear the sound of traffic on the street. But from inside the room, nothing.

He called out again, "Shiomi?" and then waited, listening, the beating of his heart the only thing breaking the quiet inside the room. When no response came, something curdled in his soul. *Face it, you stupid son of a bitch*, he thought. *She's not coming back. She never was. You got played, pure and simple.*

He considered heading back to Joe's to drown his misery with a couple of guys named Jim Beam and Jack Daniels, but you could never be sure how long Joe would stick around after closing down at 2:00 a.m. Could be a wasted drive across the city. Not that taking the Corvette for a drive was ever wasted time and besides, it wasn't like he had anything better to do.

He was surprised by just how much her betrayal hurt. In some ways, he had barely known her. In other ways, it felt like he had known her forever, their fates entwined by an intoxicating convergence of hunger and loneliness and the attraction of scarred, wounded hearts.

The ringing of his cell phone intruded on his melancholy thoughts. For a moment he hoped it was Shiomi but when he glanced at the number, he saw that it was Father Thomas. Just about the last person he wanted to talk to right now, but he knew his handler would just keep calling until he answered, so he decided to get it over with. "Yeah?"

"It's your friendly neighborhood padre," Father Thomas said. "What's with the shitty attitude?"

"Talking to you puts me in a bad mood," Malakai replied. "What do you want?"

"We need to meet."

"Not now."

"Yes, now."

"I don't have time."

"Make time. I wouldn't be calling at two o'clock in the fucking morning if this wasn't important."

"Personal or business?"

"Personal," Father Thomas said. "Life and death personal. Meet me at the church in thirty minutes."

———

When Malakai entered the abandoned church forty minutes later—he would have made it in thirty, but he detoured for a cup of coffee—he found Father Thomas standing in front of the altar. Moonlight pierced the cracks in the walls and windows and fell on the crucifix to give it an otherworldly glow. Someone had removed the guns from Christ's hands. Since he hadn't done it, he assumed Father Thomas had. Malakai didn't ask why.

He made his way to the front pew, brushed off the dust, and sat down. Father Thomas continued to stare up at the cross without moving, as if lost in a trance. Malakai noticed a burlap sack sitting on the altar. Normally he would have been curious about it, but getting burned by Shiomi had left him in a bad mood.

Bewilderment had given way to anger and now he was seriously considering tracking her down and demanding answers.

But first he had to deal with whatever shit was on Father Thomas' plate.

"Okay," he said. "I'm here. What's so damned important?"

At first he thought the ex-priest hadn't heard him, but then Father Thomas slowly turned around and asked, "Do you believe the choices we make in life are really our own?"

If Malakai had been forced to guess what question his handler might ask, that one wouldn't have made the top fifty. Maybe not even the top one hundred. It was just so random. Caught off guard, he blurted the first thing that came to mind. "Say what?"

Father Thomas continued in an almost casual tone of voice. "Are our choices really the product of free will? Or is free will just an illusion and the choices we make not really our own, but predetermined by God or fate or whatever you want to call it?"

"Predetermination is just a crutch people use to shuck responsibility for their own actions," Malakai said. "It's about as dumb as saying the devil made you do it."

"Contrary to popular opinion, the devil can't actually make anyone do anything they're not already predisposed to do," Father Thomas said. "But God... well, God can plunk your ass down in the middle of a fucked up situation where the only right thing to do is wrong."

"That why you stopped being a priest? Couldn't handle the complexities of the Almighty?"

Father Thomas looked Malakai right in the eye but it was pretty clear that he wasn't really seeing him. The classic thousand yard stare. The ex-priest's body remained in the church, but his mind was clearly someplace else. "I loved a boy," he said quietly. "Alex Orville."

Malakai did a double take. "Orville? As in Orville the farmer? The chopper guy?"

Father Thomas nodded. "Alex was his son. Cute kid, twelve years old, devoted altar boy. We became good friends and I know this isn't a popular thing to say when it comes to Catholic priests and young boys, but I loved him."

Something dark and dangerous uncoiled deep in Malakai's gut. He clenched his fists as he glared hot daggers at Father Thomas and rasped, "Tell me you're not a goddamned kiddie toucher."

That broke Father Thomas out of his glazed-over long-distance stare. His eyes pulled back from the mental horizon and glared at Malakai. "I'm not a kiddie toucher, you gutter-minded moron," he snapped. "I'm a murderer."

"You killed the kid?"

"Not the kid." Father Thomas sighed, paused to gather his thoughts, and then plunged into his story. "My first assignment as a priest was a church in the St. Petersburg area. That's where I met the Orvilles and formed my relationship with Alex. I was under the supervision of Bishop Calabrese, who had come over from Sicily. A couple months after Calabrese arrives, Alex starts acting funny. I ask him about it and he tells me Calabrese's been...touching him."

Malakai gritted his teeth so hard he thought the

enamel would crack. He despised child molesters. He would happily put a bullet between this Calabrese's eyes for free and consider it doing the world a favor.

"This was before the big church shakeup a few years back," Father Thomas continued, "when all the priest molestation cases were front page news. At the time I'm talking about, this sort of thing was hush-hush and as far as I was concerned, more of an urban legend than anything else."

"Way to go," Malakai said. "Poor kid tells you the bishop's a pervert and you don't believe him."

Father Thomas' eyes were as sad as Malakai had ever seen them, gleaming with grief and regret. "I've done a fine job of beating myself up over the years for that mistake, so I sure as hell don't need your help."

"Just saying."

"Yeah, well, how about you don't say it and just shut your damn mouth instead." Father Thomas growled before continuing his disturbing tale. "A few days later, I arrived at the church early to get ready for confession and heard some strange noises coming from the sanctuary." He swallowed hard. "When I looked around the corner, I saw... I saw Alex."

As Father Thomas told the story, Malakai unwillingly pictured it in his head. He saw the young boy bent over the altar, Calabrese standing behind him. He heard the boy's sobs, saw the boy's tears, felt the boy's shame. He decided right then and there that if Calabrese was still alive, he would hunt him down and feed him a bunch of bullets for breakfast. Some sins are just unforgiveable.

"Calabrese's hand was on the back of Alex's neck," Father Thomas said, "holding him down while he..."

His voice trembled and faded. Which was for the best. Malakai didn't need nor want to hear the graphic details.

"What did you do?" Malakai asked.

"I left."

"You didn't even try to stop it?"

"Oh, I stopped it all right," Father Thomas said grimly. "I stopped it real good. Went home, got my shotgun, and came back to confess my sins. When Calabrese came into the confessional, I said, 'Fuck you, Father, for I have sinned,' and then I blew his head off."

"You did the right thing. That sick bastard had it coming."

"Oh, he had it coming and then some. There are days I would like to dig up his corpse and kill him all over again. The Vatican covered up the murder and kept me from having to share a prison cell with some tattooed, ass-poppin' son of a bitch named Bubba, but I was still excommunicated." He looked at Malakai with haunted eyes. "Some story, huh?"

"We all have a story, Tom. How it begins isn't as important as how it ends."

"That's some pretty deep, 'Confucius says' shit right there," the ex-priest said. "So what about our story?"

"What about it?"

"Any idea how it ends?"

"It ends right here, right now. I'm starting over, new life, born again, that sort of thing."

"So I heard."

Malakai was surprised. "You did?"

"Yeah, and I even brought you a present. Because

I'm such a nice guy." Father Thomas picked up the burlap sack from the altar and tossed it to Malakai.

Malakai caught it. It was heavier than he expected. "What is it?"

"Just open the bag."

Malakai opened the sack and looked inside.

Joe's severed head stared up at him.

Malakai came out of the pew in a heartbeat, reaching for his gun. But even as he moved, he knew he was a slivered second behind the eight ball. Father Thomas already had a Kimber Solo 9mm pointed at his chest. A gun designed more for concealment than accuracy, but perfectly capable of a kill-shot at this can't-miss range.

"You son of a bitch," Malakai snarled through clenched teeth.

"Yeah, yeah, sticks and stones and all that happy horseshit," Father Thomas retorted. "If you had just been a good little boy and died when you were supposed to, Joe wouldn't have been dragged into this. Poor guy found out the hard away that it doesn't pay to be your friend."

"Why?" Malakai demanded. "Tell me why you wanted to fuck me over."

"Money," Father Thomas replied. "Cold hard cash, the root of all evil. Hey, Judas got a lousy thirty pieces of silver for selling out the Son of God. If it makes you feel any better, the Syndicate paid me a whole lot more than that for your sorry ass."

"How long?" Malakai asked. "How long have you been in their pocket?"

"Not very."

"Let me guess, you were the one who sold out Cavanaugh."

"Yeah, that was me."

"The hitter who came to my house?"

"I gave her the address."

"The ambush at The Atlantis?"

"My work as well." Father Thomas seemed almost pleased by hearing the litany of his burns and betrayals spoken aloud.

"Doesn't make sense," Malakai said. "Why go through the hassle of setting me up when you could have just killed me yourself?"

"Because I'm not a killer and killing was never part of the agreement. I'm an information broker; I sell secrets. Why do you think I wanted those photos of the senator so badly? I could have made a fortune selling those to the Syndicate." The ex-priest paused a moment to shake his head at opportunities lost, then said, "I'll put people in the crosshairs, but it's not going to be my finger that pulls the trigger."

Malakai gestured toward the gun pointed at his chest. "It's sure as hell your finger on that trigger right now, so what changed?"

"Somehow the Syndicate found out about Alex. Threatened to put a bullet in him if I didn't put one in you."

"Well," Malakai muttered, "ain't that a bitch."

"Now do you understand why you have to die?" Father Thomas asked. "Do you understand why I have to do this?"

"I understand that you jumped into bed with a bunch of snakes and now you're bitching because you got bit. What I don't understand is how Joe got wrapped up in all of this."

"The Syndicate wanted to know your whereabouts. Since you so rudely refused to tell me where you're holing up these days, I gave them Joe. Thought he might know what rock you crawled under. For what it's worth, he didn't give them anything."

"Because he didn't have anything to give." The thought of Joe suffering simply because of their friendship hurt Malakai in places he didn't know he could still hurt. It always sucked when someone else paid for your sins. "He didn't know anything."

Father Thomas shook his head in faux sadness and clucked his tongue. "Yeah. Poor Joe."

"You're an ex-priest, for God's sake!" Malakai snarled. He reached into the bag and lifted Joe's head out by the hair, shoving the death-slack face in front of his handler. "This is what you've become. A fucking murderer."

Father Thomas roared back, "I've been a murderer for a long time! Haven't you been paying attention?"

"Killing a child-molesting piece of shit priest who had it coming and killing an innocent old man are two very different things and you know it."

"I didn't kill Joe. Jesus did."

"That help you sleep at night?"

"Whiskey and hookers help me sleep at night," Father Thomas said. "Say what you want, but Jesus killed Joe, not me."

"Semantics, you son of a bitch."

As the last word left his lips, Malakai made his move, hurling Joe's decapitated head at Father Thomas. The gruesome projectile struck the Kimber and knocked the pistol out of the ex-priest's hand. Joe's head thunked to the floor with a meaty thud and rolled to a stop against the base of the altar. The half-open eyes stared up at the ceiling as if begging Heaven why this had happened.

Malakai shucked his .45 with the speed of a cobra strike and pointed it at Father Thomas' chest. He felt ice in his veins and projected the coldness with his eyes, letting the ex-priest know there was about to be some hell to pay. "Now it's *my* finger on the trigger, asshole."

Strangely, Father Thomas evidenced no fear, just bitter relief and desolate resignation. "Go ahead," he said. "Do it. My life turned to shit a long time ago. I'm ready to knock on Heaven's door and see if God will still let me in."

"Ten bucks says God would spit right in your face, but you're never gonna get the chance to find out. You aren't getting off that easy."

"What's that supposed to mean?"

"Me killing you is nothing more than vengeance," said Malakai. "What I want from you is something else entirely. The next level, you might say."

Father Thomas' brow furrowed. "What are you talking about?"

"Penance." Malakai gave the word the ominous edge it deserved. "A good little Catholic boy like yourself ought to know that you have to pay for your sins."

"My sins are forgiven."

Malakai jerked his chin toward the crucifix hanging on the wall. "By Him maybe, but I haven't forgiven jack-shit. I want an act of contrition."

"Like what?"

"Pick up your gun. Use your left hand."

"You're kidding, right?"

Malakai narrowed his eyes until they were nothing but glittering slits in the moonlight. "Does it look like I'm in a kidding mood right now? Pick up the gun."

Father Thomas hesitated for a moment, then leaned over and picked up the gun with his left hand. He kept his finger far away from the trigger, no doubt fully aware that he didn't have a chance in hell of getting off a shot before Malakai drilled him about a dozen times.

"Good boy," Malakai said. "Now put the barrel in your mouth, suck down hard, and pull the trigger."

Shock and fear crawled across Father Thomas' face. "I can't kill myself! It's a cardinal sin!"

"Exactly," Malakai replied, his tone harder and harsher than the hollow-points in his gun. "A one-way ride on a fast train to Hell. Isn't that how you put it? You picked the wrong guy to fuck over, Tommy."

Father Thomas started to panic. Malakai could see it all over his face and hear it in his voice. "Please, man, I'm begging you, just kill me. If I take my own life, I'm damned beyond all hope. If you do it, at least I have a chance."

"Fuck that. You deserve to burn in Hell for what you did."

"For the love of God, show some fucking mercy!"

"Fresh out. You're gonna eat that bullet."

Desperate, believing his soul was at stake, Father Thomas blurted, "How about a trade? I have information about Shiomi."

Malakai felt his heartbeat quicken. "What about her?"

"I can tell you why she never came back last night."

"So tell me."

The ex-priest shook his head. "Not until you take suicide off the table. I'll tell you what happened to Shiomi when you tell me that the bullet that kills me will come from your hand, not mine. I've got no problem letting you have your vengeance, but eternal damnation? That's a bit much to ask."

Malakai didn't think about it long. Sure, the traitorous ex-priest might just be spinning a lie to get what he wanted, but Malakai knew he needed to hear him out. When it came to Shiomi, he could take no chances.

"Fine," he said. "Assuming your information isn't bullshit, you've got a deal."

The relief on Father Thomas' face was nearly comical and Malakai realized the man had nearly crapped his pants at the thought of committing suicide. Apparently the thought of being eternally slow-roasted on the devil's spit had a way of loosening the bowels.

"It's not bullshit," the ex-priest said. "Tanaka found out about you and Shiomi and had a couple of his goons intercept her last night on her way back to you. She's being held at the mansion."

"Give me the address."

Father Thomas rattled it off, then added, "Needless to say, Tanaka was not happy to hear that his daughter is playing Romeo and Juliet with his enemy."

"I wasn't his enemy until right now," Malakai said. "I was just a guy doing a job."

"Somehow I doubt those kind of semantics are bringing Shiomi much comfort right now. Thanks to you, Tanaka disowned her, hung her in chains, and told his soldiers they could do whatever they wanted to the bitch." Father Thomas chuckled coldly. "Bet those

Syndicate boys had a real good time last night playing with your precious whore."

Rage consumed Malakai. He knew he was being baited into pulling the trigger, but he didn't care. He gave the ex-priest exactly what he wanted.

Right between the eyes.

Father Thomas' head snapped back from the point-blank impact as the bullet blew open the back of his skull. Gore arced up and splattered across the crucifix. The wet blood dripped down the impaled Christ and lent an air of realism to the statue. For just a fraction of a moment, Malakai could have sworn that the crucified Savior turned His head and gazed down with sorrowful eyes at His fallen child crumpled on the floor. Probably just a trick of the moonlight.

Malakai suddenly realized he had been holding his breath. He exhaled, a long, shuddering sigh, and sat down on the pew. He stayed there for several moments, just staring down at Father Thomas' corpse, and then raised his eyes to the blood-spattered cross hanging on the wall. His faith had been royally fucked up by a dangerously zealous father, but Malakai still believed there was a God, and he couldn't help but wonder what that God thought of what he had just done.

The moment of reflection was just that—a moment —and then his mind returned to the more pressing concern of Shiomi. Ponderings about redemption, damnation, and all the shades of gray in between would have to wait until she was safe. Attempting to rescue her from the fortified Syndicate estate of her father might prove to be a suicide mission, but so be it. Leaving her there simply was not an option.

He might be nothing more than a hired gun, an ice-veined killer, but with her, he felt like something more. Something better. And when they were together and he gazed into Shiomi's eyes, he knew that with him, she no longer thought of herself as a whore. She healed him and he healed her and they both needed the other to tame the scars on their souls. He would either save her... or die trying.

But first he had to figure out how to infiltrate the Syndicate estate.

As it turned out, Father Thomas might have provided him a way.

Not giving a damn about desecrating the dead—especially a dead asshole who had betrayed him—Malakai rifled through the priest's pockets. He pulled out three condom wrappers, a bag of weed, and a travel-sized tube of lubricant before he found what he was looking for—Father Thomas' cell phone.

He scrolled through the contacts until he found one labeled FARMER. He knew it was late—or early, depending on your point of view—but with Shiomi's life on the line, he didn't care. He called the number.

Someone answered on the sixth ring with a sleepy, "Hello?"

"Is this Orville?"

"Depends on who's asking."

"You don't know my name, but you gave me a ride the other day."

"I give lots of rides," Orville said, instantly cautious.

"I was the one with a bullet hole in my shoulder."

"How did you get this number?"

"Tom's phone."

"Where's Tom?"

"Dead."

"Dead?" Orville sounded like he couldn't believe what he had just heard.

"Yeah," Malakai confirmed. "Dead."

"How?"

"I killed him."

Next came a long pause as Orville digested the news before he asked, "Care to give me a reason?"

"He asked me to."

"Why?"

"Guilt," said Malakai.

Another long pause. Malakai waited it out. Finally Orville sighed. "Well, Tom certainly had a lot of that. He tell ya what he did for my boy?"

"Yeah, he told me."

"Good," Orville said. "Now give me your word you'll never mention it again."

"You have my word."

"Appreciate that. Now, what do you need from me?"

"A ride."

"Where ya going?"

"To war," Malakai said grimly.

CHAPTER 18

THREE HOURS LATER, Malakai stood in the cargo bay of Orville's UH-1 with a parachute strapped to his back and shifted his balance as the farmer banked the chopper through the pre-dawn sky, heading toward the Syndicate mansion. He couldn't see the altimeter, but he knew they were somewhere around 10,000 feet. Not the highest jump he had ever made, but it was certainly up there. He looked over Orville's shoulder and out the windshield as wispy clouds scuttled by like disinterested ghosts.

Malakai was garbed in black, a tactical vest holding his FNX-45 pistol, a Ka-Bar combat knife, assorted grenades, and extra magazines for both the sidearm and the Heckler & Koch UMP-45 submachine gun slung across his chest. There was a whole lot of killing strapped to his body and he knew he would most likely need every bit of it to survive this mission.

He had almost called Asher to back him up on the strike. A rock 'em, sock 'em two-man army of destruction, just like the old days. But two things had stopped him.

The first was simply a matter of time constraints, of the numbers running down toward zero way too fast. He knew Asher would come if he asked for help—they were friends, brothers in arms, and would always be there for each other when the stakes were down and the shit hit the fan—but it would take him too long to travel from Mexico to Miami. With Shiomi's life in immediate danger, Malakai couldn't afford to wait.

Secondly, this might very well be a suicide mission. Malakai knew there was a good chance that he would die trying to get Shiomi back. It was a risk he was willing to take, a price he was willing to pay. But Asher had just found peace again, had walked away from the killing game to be with Larissa. Malakai couldn't ask him to throw that away.

Asher had fought his battle alone, had gone to war and spilled blood for a chance at a new life with the woman he loved.

Now it was time for Malakai to do the same.

Orville turned his head and yelled over the roar of the rotors, "For the record, I still think this is a stupid idea."

"No choice," Malakai yelled back. "I have to get to Shiomi and the place is too well-fortified for a direct assault. I need to catch them off guard, take 'em by surprise, so a HALO insertion is my best bet."

"High altitude, low opening jumps ain't no joke."

"I'll be fine."

"Until your boots hit the ground and you get your butt blown to bits by the bad guys."

Thinking about Shiomi suffering God-knew-what

at the hands of her ruthless father and his loyal-to-the-death minions, Malakai said, "I have to try."

"Yeah, I know. Love makes fools of us all." Orville shook his head. "Get ready. Target's just up ahead."

Malakai pulled on a pair of black shooting gloves and goggles, then slid open the door. The cold wind rushed into the cargo bay and buffeted him so badly that he rocked back on his heels. He leaned into the wind, steadying his balance.

"Ten seconds!" Orville called out. "You're gonna need God and all the angels to get through this one."

"Then pray they're not busy."

"Amen to that. Five seconds to target."

Malakai braced his hands on each side of the door, not sure if he was being brave or stupid. Such a thin line between courage and insanity.

"Four. Three. Two. One. Go!"

No more thought, no hesitation. Shiomi needed him and that's all that mattered.

Malakai leaped out of the chopper, armed to the teeth and ready to kill in the name of love.

———

The two soldiers conducting a perimeter sweep of the Syndicate estate paused by the southeast corner of the mansion for a cigarette break. Sentry #1 flicked open a Zippo, fired up his cancer stick, and then reached over to light up Sentry #2.

As his partner applied the flame to the tip of his cigarette, Sentry #2 said, "You know we're breaking one of the first rules of nighttime guard duty, don't you?"

"What do you mean?" Sentry #1 snapped the Zippo shut and shoved it back in his pocket.

"Lighting up. Big no-no. Flame from the lighter screws up your night vision and the glow at the end of your cigarette makes you a target. Don't you read Tom Clancy?"

"I'm more of a *Penthouse* kind of guy," Sentry #1 replied. "Besides, this is the Syndicate mansion. Who'd be stupid enough to attack it?"

Most prey is not conditioned to look skyward for predators, so neither man thought to look up for threats. They failed to notice the black-garbed invader floating toward the ground above and behind them, skillfully controlling his descent with the steering toggles of his chute.

Sentry #2 said, "Man, can you believe the boss using his own daughter as bait? That's a special kind of cold, man."

"Yeah, I agree," his partner said. "But the way I hear it, the whore had it coming."

"You take a turn with her last night?"

"Of course. You?"

"Hell, yeah, I did."

They both heard a rustling noise behind them at the same time. They cut the chitchat and turned, cigarettes jutting from between their lips.

In the last few seconds of their lives, they saw Malakai twenty feet above them, chute flared like the wings of a black hawk. His .45 was already out, bucking in his fist as he emptied half a magazine into them. The suppressor reduced the shots to muffled coughs in the pre-dawn darkness.

The sentries never knew what hit them. The bullets smashed into their chests, necks, and faces, the downward firing angle ensuring shattered spines. Both bodies hit the grass a few seconds before Malakai's feet touched down, thankful to be on solid ground again.

He quickly hid the parachute behind some shrubs, peeled off the goggles, and performed a quick weapons check. He had entered the dragon's den and his chances of survival were damn slim unless his arsenal was cocked, locked, and ready to rock.

He performed a tactical magazine exchange, swapping the half-spent mag for a full one as he scanned his surroundings. He watched and listened, waiting to see if anyone had detected his aerial intrusion. No cries of alarm, no warning shouts. So far, so good.

He almost didn't see the two Dobermans that swarmed out of the shadows. They appeared as if by magic, coalescing from the darkness. He glimpsed them at the last possible moment. The lead dog lunged for his throat. The second dog came in low. The speed and coordination of the attack showed sophisticated training that Malakai might have admired if they hadn't been trying to kill him.

He threw himself sideways. An instinctive, graceless maneuver, but it worked. The first Doberman's fangs snapped shut an inch from his cheek as it sailed past.

The second dog's teeth crunched down on the pistol's sound-suppressor, nearly wrenching the weapon out of Malakai's hand. The Doberman whipped its head from side to side, thrashing like a rabid wolf, turning the suppressor into useless junk.

Malakai pulled the trigger and the dog's head exploded, turned inside out by the point-blank power of a .45 slug. With the suppressor too damaged to actually suppress the sonics, the sound of the shot whip-cracked through the pre-dawn silence. Not good.

Malakai rolled onto his back as the remaining Doberman lunged for him again. A single bullet to the brisket put the beast down. This time the shot sounded even louder. Looked like the gods of war had just taken a big, steaming shit all over his element of surprise.

He got back on his feet, removed the scrap-metal remains of the suppressor from the FNX, and shoved it back in its holster, replacing it with the H&K UMP. He made sure the sub-gun was ready for some full auto rock and roll and then ran toward the front of the mansion, eyes peeled for hostiles.

———

Seated in his office as he examined some papers, Tanaka heard the two shots from outside, the second one louder than the first but both clearly identifiable as gunshots. A smile creased his lips. His plan had worked. The trap was sprung. The foolish American assassin had come to rescue Shiomi.

It amazed him how easily he had ceased thinking of her as his daughter. She had betrayed him, defied him, broken Syndicate rules, and now she held no value other than a piece of abused meat laid out to lure a mad dog to his death.

Yoshi rushed into the office without knocking, a sure sign he was distressed. "Apparently Father Thomas failed to take care of our problem."

From somewhere outside came the staccato sound of a submachine gun ripping off rounds.

"So it would seem," said Tanaka. "The lesson here is never send a man of God to do the devil's work."

"Father Thomas was no man of God," Yoshi replied. "He was just a well-paid Judas."

"Perhaps, but he served his purpose." Tanaka paused for a moment, then asked, "How many men do we have on the premises?"

Yoshi ticked off the numbers on his fingers. "Two at the front gate, two patrolling the grounds, and eight off-duty personnel in the barracks. And, of course, Jesus."

"Always good to have Jesus on your side," Tanaka smirked.

He pulled open a desk drawer and took out a gold-plated Desert Eagle .50. He handed the massive hand cannon to Yoshi, who looked like he would rather be holding a dead baby than the gigantic pistol. Probably afraid the recoil would break his wrist.

"I am going to get Shiomi," Tanaka said. "Jesus will accompany me. You will remain here. Assuming he survives the guards outside and makes it this far, Malakai has to go down this hallway to reach the pool room. When he does, you can ambush him."

Tanaka turned and lifted the *wakizashi* sword from its cradle, then headed for the door.

Yoshi stared at the gun in his hand for a moment, then lifted troubled eyes to his master. "Sir, I don't think I can—"

Tanaka interrupted, "Yoshi, the Americans have a phrase that I am quite fond of but rarely find occasion to use."

"And what would that be, sir?"

"Don't be a fucking pussy."

Tanaka slammed the door shut behind him. The last thing he saw was Yoshi's miserable face staring down at the Desert Eagle in his trembling hands.

———

Malakai heard the fountain burbling at the front of the mansion a second before he rounded the corner and saw it. He spotted two sentries—since they were hoofing it up the driveway, he presumed they were coming from the front gate—on the opposite side of the fountain. Without breaking stride, Malakai fired on the run. His bullets whipped through the tower of water and tore into the sentries' torsos. The two men spun to the ground in scarlet sprays.

He sprinted up the mansion's front steps and took cover behind a porch column taller than a giraffe and thicker than an elephant's leg. Peering around the column and through the narrow windows framing each side of the front door, he saw eight enemy gunmen rushing into the cavernous foyer, every one of them packing Vector SMGs. Every one of them ready to kill, every one of them ready to die if necessary.

As Malakai watched from behind the pillar, two of the gunners peeled off from the others and cautiously approached the door.

Looked like now was as good a time as any to knock.

He plucked a grenade from his vest, pulled the pin, and tossed it toward the door. He ducked back behind the column as the blast rocked the air and blew apart the door. He paused for a moment to ride out the wave of shrapnel and debris, then spun into action.

He one-handed his UMP as he dove over the shredded corpses of the two gunman, using his other hand to grab one of the dead men's Vector as he went by. He landed in the gritty, smoke-filled foyer and instantly threw himself forward in a somersault as gunfire erupted. He came up in a combat crouch with the UMP in one hand, sweeping left to the right, and the Vector in the other, sweeping right to left.

Bullets burned the air in a seething maelstrom of lead and steel.

Malakai's guns instantly cut down two Syndicate soldiers, the high-velocity impacts dropping them in twitching heaps. He kept the triggers at full throttle, brass spitting from the ejection ports. Another gunner went down, punched backward by a trio of .45 slugs to the sternum.

There were bullets everywhere and they were not all his. Return fire tracked his way. A round scorched past his cheek like a hot kiss from the Reaper. Malakai rolled to the side, still firing. Another bad guy bit the dust with his skull popped open.

Only two left, but Malakai knew he was pushing the razor-thin edges of his luck. Enemy bullets pounded the floor all around him, peppering him with fragments. The gods of war could turn on him at any second. The bastards were fickle like that.

He threw himself backward, coming up against the wall. The last three bullets from his Vector sent one of the soldiers ducking for cover behind a huge floor vase. The other gunner was slower and the final triple-burst from the H&K UMP chopped open his chest in bloody spurts.

Both submachine guns empty, Malakai let them

drop and drew his FNX-45 before either one hit the floor.

With Malakai's sub-guns silenced, the sole surviving soldier must have assumed he was unarmed. The foolish gunman popped up from behind the vase and started to draw a bead. He instantly realized his mistake. His eyes went wide when he saw the .45 in Malakai's fist pointed right at him. Then his eyes went dead as a bullet bored a hole right between them.

Malakai watched the man go down with the back of his head blown open, then holstered his pistol, retrieved the UMP, slapped in a fresh magazine, and moved toward the long hallway that stretched before him.

Hang on, Shiomi. I'm coming for you.

He had just killed eight men for her.

He would kill eight hundred if that's what it took.

———

Inside Tanaka's office, Yoshi watched on the CCTV monitors as Malakai shot the last soldier in the head. As he saw the man's bullet-scrambled brains explode out the back of his skull, Yoshi's hand began to shake even worse than before. Sweat sheeted down his face. He licked his lips and tasted the salty tang of his fear. He had never been so terrified in all his life.

The Syndicate had always been his shield, his safety, his protector. But now the Syndicate was under attack by a man who seemed ruthless, relentless, and unstoppable. Malakai had just decimated the mansion's guard force and Yoshi had no doubt that he would be decimated too.

Unless he killed Malakai first.

He watched on the monitor as the assassin crept stealthily down the hallway, unknowingly drawing closer to Yoshi's position.

Yoshi aimed the Desert Eagle at the door, using both badly-shaking hands to heft the heavy pistol. It felt like it weighed approximately the same as a concrete block. His eyes flicked back and forth between the door and the monitor, tracking Malakai's progress down the hall. He silently prayed to Buddha, his ancestors, and anyone else out there listening in the cosmos that he survived his coming encounter with one of the most lethal killers on the planet.

——————

Tanaka stood by the pool, Shiomi beside him, hands bound behind her back with chains. He could hear the sound of gunfire from the other end of the mansion, faint but furious, as the dorsal fins of the tiger sharks sliced the surface of the water behind him.

"It appears to be true love after all," Tanaka sneered. "Your boyfriend has entered the jaws of the lion to get you back."

"You're not a lion," Shiomi snapped. "You're a cockroach, and Malakai is going to stomp the shit out of you."

Tanaka gave her a wintry stare. She made it so easy to hate her. "You know, last night Jesus asked me if he could cut out your tongue and I said no, but in hindsight, perhaps I should have allowed it."

He pulled a butterfly knife from his pocket—he had

given the sword to Jesus—and with a flick of his wrist flipped open the blade. Light reflected off the pool water and skittered along the razored edge.

"You know why I denied him? Not because of any lingering emotions I might still feel for you, because trust me, I do not. No, I told him I needed your tongue intact so you could scream for me when the time came." He leaned in close, like a father about to impart some very crucial wisdom to his daughter. "You are bait, Shiomi, and the best kind of bait is bloody—"

Without warning, he stabbed the knife into the meat of her thigh.

"—and screams like hell."

He twisted the blade.

Blood spurted.

Shiomi screamed.

———

Malakai heard the screams and felt his heart freeze. The horrible cries came from behind the large door at the end of the hallway. Several other doors led off the corridor to adjacent rooms. Caution dictated that he check them all to avoid leaving an enemy at his back, but he didn't have the time. His need to get to Shiomi trumped combat protocols. While he wasted time kicking in each and every door, Shiomi might very well be getting killed. He could not take that risk. Sometimes you just had to follow the pull of your heart instead of the voice in your head. Sometimes love has no choice but to be reckless.

He rushed down the hall toward the door at the end.

On the CCTV monitors, Yoshi watched Malakai surge down the hall like a force of nature that would not, could not, be stopped. But stopping him was exactly what Yoshi had been ordered to do. Never once had he disobeyed an order from Tanaka and today would not be the day he started.

He aimed the Desert Eagle at the door and used the monitors to gauge when to fire.

Now!

He yanked the trigger.

The gun roared and the massive recoil hurled the muzzle toward the ceiling.

Had he been running a half-second faster, Malakai would have caught the .50 caliber brain-crusher right in the temple. Instead, it blew through the door and burned a scorching path of superheated air less than a centimeter from the tip of his nose.

He reacted instantly, throwing himself sideways, ramming his shoulder against the door, smashing it open.

He saw a man—based on conversations with Shiomi, he assumed it was her father's servant—fumbling to bring a Desert Eagle back under control.

Yoshi never stood a chance. Far too slow, far too late.

Malakai cut loose with the UMP, stitching a salvo of .45 slugs across Yoshi's stomach. He folded over as the bullets punched into his guts. Malakai went for the quick kill, putting his next burst into the top of Yoshi's exposed head, shattering the thick skull-bone into splinters. Yoshi was dead before his corpse even hit the floor.

Threat neutralized, Malakai spun out of the doorway and back into the hallway. The combat clock in the back of his mind ran down the numbers. It had only taken a handful of seconds to eliminate Yoshi, but those seconds might be the difference between life and death for Shiomi. Her screams had been full of pain and the fact that she hadn't screamed again brought him no comfort.

He raced down the corridor, ignoring the doors on either side, wholly focused on the door at the end. Somewhere behind that door, Shiomi suffered. That door could have been the main gate of Hell, and Malakai would have torn it off its hinges on his way through.

He was almost there when the last door on the left burst open and Jesus Twin barreled out like a rabid rhino, armed with a *wakizashi* sword.

Malakai tried to bring the UMP into play, but Jesus used the sword like a baseball bat and clubbed the subgun to the floor. Malakai let it go and reached for his pistol, but as soon as it cleared leather, Jesus slapped that out of his hand too.

"No guns, *cabron*," the Hispanic hitman snarled. "If I wanted a goddamned gunfight, I wouldn't be holding this pig-sticker, now would I?" He licked his lips in what could only be described as predatory anticipation. "Steel to steel, *mano-a-mano*, that's how it's gonna be, so I can cut you apart piece by piece for what you did to my brother."

"Have it your way." Malakai unsheathed his Ka-Bar. "Story still ends with you dead."

Jesus looked at the Ka-Bar's seven-inch blade and chuckled. "Mine's bigger."

"Size is overrated."

"All depends on where you stick it." Jesus lunged forward without warning, swinging the sword in a vicious overhand strike that would have split Malakai's skull like a melon had it struck.

But Malakai had been expecting just such a dirty trick—he suffered no delusions that this would be a clean fight—and was ready for it. He deflected the blow to the side and then countered with a wicked back-slash that flayed Jesus' right cheek wide open. Crimson beaded in the wound.

Jesus hissed in pain. The Ka-Bar had sliced through his skin like a hot knife through soft butter. He touched a hand to his face, then looked at the blood staining his fingers. His visage twisted with rage. "I swear by all that is fucking holy," he growled, "that's the last drop of blood you get out of me."

Malakai remained balanced on the balls of his feet, knife at the ready. "Wishful thinker, hey? I admire that in an asshole."

Where Malakai was deadly grace and lethal finesse, Jesus was all raging bull. He bellowed to give voice to his anger and then attacked in a series of rapid sword strikes. The sheer ferocity drove Malakai backward, forcing him to yield to Jesus' wrecking ball fury. He hated to retreat even a single step. Hated moving further away from Shiomi instead of toward her. But right now there was nothing he could do but play defense and wait for an opening. As long as he didn't fall to the sword, he knew Jesus would give him an opportunity to strike back. He just had to survive the bludgeoning assault.

Easier said than done.

The *wakizashi* stabbed, slashed, and flicked like a silver serpent's tongue. Malakai parried the blows as best he could, but in a sword-versus-knife fight, it is inevitable that the sword's longer reach will draw blood, no matter how good the guy with the knife is. Malakai's Ka-Bar blocked most of the blows, but Jesus was a brutal madman who knew how to wield the *wakizashi* and Malakai's arms were soon laced with numerous, stinging cuts. More scars for the collection.

"Who's bleeding now, *cabron?*" Jesus rasped, aiming a short, fast, sideways strike designed to horizontally bisect his opponent's skull.

Malakai expertly deflected the blow with the Ka-Bar. "If that's the best you got, get ready to say hello to your brother in Hell."

"I haven't even begun to give you my best," Jesus retorted. "I'm a fucking cat toying with a mouse. If I wanted you dead, you would be dead already." He launched another strike and steel clashed as sword and knife met yet again. "But killing you quick isn't half as fun as killing you slow. I'm going to rip the flesh from your bones piece by piece for what you did to Joseph."

Malakai slashed at Jesus' chest, but the big Hispanic danced out of the way, lighter on his feet than would seem possible for a man of his stature. "Hey, shithead," Malakai said, "when are you going to wake up and face the fact that your brother was nothing more than a little bitch?"

"Funny you should mention bitch," Jesus fired back, "'cause I fucked yours last night and that little whore loved it."

Malakai abruptly decided that defense was over-rated. He powered forward at full speed, lunging with the knife, driving the blade toward Jesus' face. When the Hispanic hitman raised the sword to block the blow, Malakai adjusted his attack. He came in low and smashed the top of his head into Jesus' gut.

Jesus grunted as the wind exploded out of him, but the blow was hardly incapacitating. Even through his gasps, he managed to slam the sword's hilt down on Malakai's spine. His combat vest absorbed enough of the impact to prevent his vertebrae from shattering, but it was still a powerful blow. Pain blazed through Malakai's nervous system and he fell heavily to his knees directly in front of Jesus, like a condemned sinner bowing before his executioner.

Smiling in anticipated victory, Jesus pulled the *wakizashi* back for a decapitating strike. Between his strength and the blade's sharpness, he would no doubt need only a single blow to separate Malakai's head from his shoulders.

But Malakai was not nearly as helpless as he feigned. He had just needed to get in close to Jesus, where the sword's length worked against it. The *wakizashi* was perfect if you could keep your victim at arm's length. But this close, the knife was the superior weapon.

He slammed the heavy blade of the Ka-Bar into the side of Jesus' right knee. Bone ruptured with a sound like breaking glass and Jesus shrieked. Moving with lethal and rapid precision, Malakai ripped out the knife and slashed the razor edge down across the back of Jesus' left ankle, severing the Achilles tendon. The lightning fast pair of knife-strikes left Jesus completely crippled. The giant came tumbling down.

The sword fell from his spasming fingers as he started to collapse on top of Malakai. Anticipating the action, Malakai caught the falling man, flipped him around, and slammed him down on his back in one fluid move. He snatched up the sword and then straddled Jesus' barrel-sized chest, knife in one hand, sword in the other. He crossed both blades against his enemy's throat. He could see veins pulsing frantically just beneath the skin as his muscles tensed for the killing stroke.

In desperation, Jesus cried out, "Wait!"

"Give me one good reason."

"I'm begging you! Please, don't kill me. I don't want to die."

Malakai had seen it countless times before. Just another bully who turned into a coward when his moment came to pay the Reaper. "You're already dead," he rasped. "You were dead the moment you touched her."

"You don't have to do this. You and me, we're killers. But even killers can show mercy sometimes."

Malakai was done wasting time on this asshole. "You know," he said, "I could, but there's just one question you have to ask yourself."

"What's that?"

Malakai bared his teeth in a savage grin. "What would Jesus do?"

He whipped his arms outward like a conductor

leading an orchestra. Both blades slashed through Jesus' throat and unleashed a wicked spray of blood.

Malakai didn't wait to see Jesus' eyes glaze over in death. As the man gurgled and gasped his final seconds away, Malakai dropped the *wakizashi* next to the twitching body and then shoved the Ka-Bar back into its sheath. He retrieved and holstered his .45, then picked up the H&K UMP and jogged over to the door at the end of the corridor. He never gave Jesus another glance. Just tucked the submachine gun tight to his shoulder and went through the door, eyes locked onto his sights, seeking targets.

The first thing he saw was Tanaka standing beside a humongous swimming pool, Shiomi wrapped in chains beside him. He had a Springfield XDS-9 automatic tucked against her temple and kept her body between him and Malakai as a shield. Blood streamed down Shiomi's leg from a stab wound in her thigh. The sight enraged Malakai but he forced himself to stay cool. He needed a clear head to extract Shiomi from this dangerous situation. Now was not the time to let his primal emotions seize the reins.

When she saw him, Shiomi cried out, "Shoot him!"

Malakai calculated the odds in less than a second. All he could see was the top half of Tanaka's head and the hand holding the gun to her temple. Everything else was hidden behind the daughter he had disowned. Malakai silently cursed the gutless coward. He glanced down at the UMP in his hands, running the numbers in his head.

"He can't shoot me," Tanaka said. "He picked the wrong tool for the job. A submachine gun lacks the precision necessary for a clean headshot. He must also bear in mind that not even a headshot guarantees a favorable outcome, because it is quite possible that my death spasms would convulse my finger on the trigger and put a bullet through your brain as well." He smiled coldly. "In other words, if he kills me, he kills you."

Malakai was already tired of listening to this bastard talk. He made a decision. "You forgot one thing," he said.

Tanaka smirked. "And what would that be?"

Unseen by the crime lord, Malakai thumbed the UMP's selector switch to single-shot mode and replied, "I'm downright surgical with this bad boy."

He fired and the bullet hit the third knuckle of Tanaka's trigger finger, shattering the joint, making it impossible for him to shoot. The .45 slug nearly chopped the digit clean off, leaving it dangling from Tanaka's hand by only a ragged thread of skin.

As soon as the sound of the shot whip-cracked through the cavernous room, Shiomi snapped her head back sharply, smashing her father's nose. He staggered back and she rammed him with her shoulder, pushing him toward the pool. He flailed, off balance, heels dangling over the edge. She rammed him again and he tumbled backward. But as he fell, he managed to grab the chain wrapped around her wrists and pulled her into the pool with him. They both hit the water with a loud splash.

Malakai rushed forward. "Shiomi!"

The weight of the chains dragged her under. The stab wound in her thigh leaked blood into the water in an expanding cloud of crimson.

A few yards away, Tanaka flailed and spluttered

like a drowning toddler. "Help! I can't swim! Help!" Panic honed a jagged edge on his voice.

The sharks appeared from out of nowhere, four torpedo-shaped shadows silently cruising toward the fresh prey that had fallen into their aquatic domain.

At the bottom of the pool, Shiomi struggled against her chains. Her long black hair floated around her head in twisted tangles as she thrashed about.

Heart pounding, Malakai started to dive in after her, but pulled up short as the sharks ghosted into view. Sharks were bad enough, but their presence was compounded by his crippling affliction, his ichthyophobia. His rational fear of sharks and his irrational fear of fish—and a shark is the biggest damn fish of them all—conspired to keep him from throwing himself into the pool after Shiomi. He wanted to...but he just couldn't do it.

"Damn it!" he snarled. He had never hated himself more than he did right now. He leveled the UMP at the sharks and emptied the magazine. "Get away from her!"

He saw lines of bubbles as the bullets punched down through the water, but the sharks kept coming. Driven by their prehistoric instincts, they started circling Shiomi and Tanaka.

Malakai tossed aside the empty sub-gun with a snarled curse.

A conflict raged within. Fear overwhelmed him, nailed his feet to the floor. But his feelings for Shiomi were just as strong and he desperately wanted to leap into the water and try to rescue her. It was a battle between his mind and his heart.

Shiomi looked up at him from the bottom of the

pool, terror etched on her face, eyes begging him to save her.

One of the sharks peeled away from the others and surged toward her. Malakai watched in horror as the serrated teeth snapped shut on Shiomi's left leg and severed it just below the knee. Blood jetted from the ragged stump as the shark darted away, jaws working furiously as it chomped on its gruesome meal.

"No!" Malakai cried out.

In an instant, the heart won.

Love conquered fear.

He dove into the pool.

As his body knifed through the water, another shark angled in for an attack, mouth agape.

Malakai drew the .45 and fired a shot directly into the shark's eye. The half-blinded beast turned away, thrashing its head from side to side, blood streaming from the exploded socket.

Malakai swam the rest of the way to Shiomi, hoping he wasn't too late. Her face was a mask of pain and terror. Blood loss from her severed leg was going to be a problem real quick but the first priority was getting her some air. He pressed his mouth to hers and blew desperately-needed breath into her lungs.

When he pulled back, she looked over his shoulder and her eyes went wide as saucers.

He spun around to see one of the sharks speeding toward them. He shoved Shiomi out of the way and rolled away from the attack, the adrenalin surging through his system helping him move faster underwater than normal. The predator's teeth snapped shut an inch from his face. As the shark whipped past, its pectoral fin hit Malakai's hand, knocking the pistol from his grasp.

He grabbed at it but missed and the gun sank to the bottom of the pool.

The shark circled around for another attack.

With no other options, Malakai unsheathed the Ka-Bar as the shark zeroed in like an underwater missile, fifteen feet of primal killing power.

Knife versus shark, Malakai thought. *What could go wrong?*

At the last possible second, he threw himself backward. Again the snapping jaws missed his flesh by millimeters. He doubted he would get so lucky a third time. He needed to end this right here and now.

As the shark passed over him, Malakai rammed the Ka-Bar deep into the vulnerable underbelly. He buried it to the hilt and the shark's own momentum dragged the blade through its guts. Entrails spilled out all over Malakai in a hot, gushing burst.

He shook off the slimy gore and swam back to Shiomi, who was losing blood fast from the stump of her leg. But at least she was still conscious. From the corner of his eye, he saw the wounded shark flee to the other end of the pool. But its brethren sharks, intoxicated by the copious blood and bile spilling from the belly wound, turned on it in a prehistoric frenzy. Within seconds, they churned the water into crimson foam.

With the sharks momentarily distracted, Malaki hauled Shiomi to the surface. She gasped in huge mouthfuls of air, sucking precious oxygen into her starving lungs.

Malakai helped her to the edge of the pool. She clung there for a moment as he hopped out, then he took her hand and pulled her to safety, laying her down on her back. The sight of her ragged leg stump enraged and shamed him. If only he had jumped in sooner, it might never have happened. She had paid the price for his fear and cowardice. If she survived, Malakai would spend the rest of his days doing his damnedest to make it up to her.

But first he had to save her life.

In the pool, the sharks continued to feed on one of their own in a seething mass of fins and fury.

Just a few yards away from the feeding frenzy, Tanaka sputtered and flailed, trying to stay afloat. "Help! Somebody! Help me! Please!"

Malakai ignored him, wholly focused on Shiomi. Right now she was the only thing that mattered. If he didn't get the bleeding stopped, he would lose her and all this would have been for nothing. He had killed fourteen men tonight—fifteen, if you counted Father Thomas—but if Shiomi died too, then it wasn't a fair trade.

Her eyes started to glaze. "Malakai..." Her voice sounded weak and frail.

"Don't talk," he said. "Save your strength. I have to find a way to stop the bleeding."

In the pool, a shark's tail-fin struck Tanaka in the face. It made a loud slapping sound, but not as loud as Tanaka's terrified shrieks.

Malakai's head swiveled, scanning the area for something, anything, he could use to stanch the blood pulsing from Shiomi's severed leg. He spotted the alcove nearby. "I'll be right back," he said.

He ran into the small room and saw the chainsaw and blowtorch. He had no doubt that this was the room where Joe died, but now was not the time to indulge his grief.

He grabbed the blowtorch and rushed back to Shiomi. She looked up at him with frightened eyes as blue flame hissed from the nozzle.

He hated to hurt her, but there was no other choice. "You want something to bite down on? This is gonna hurt like hell."

She shook her head. "Just do it."

Malakai nodded and applied the flame to the stump, cauterizing the ghastly wound, burning shut the severed veins and arteries. Shiomi bravely gritted her teeth against the pain. It felt like forever before he could turn off the torch, but finally the bleeding stopped, the stump now charred and blackened. Smoke rose up in little wisps.

Shiomi coughed and wrinkled her nose in disgust. "God, what's that smell?"

"Burnt flesh," Malakai replied, dragging the back of his wrist across his brow to wipe away sweat. "Either that or I shit myself when I had to jump in with those damn sharks."

She gave him an exhausted smile. "Well, I'm glad you did."

"You're glad I shit myself?"

"No, I'm glad you came for me."

He leaned over and hovered with his lips just an inch from hers. "Of course I came for you," he said, then erased that inch of separation.

Tanaka's shrieking interrupted the kiss. "Help! Somebody help me! Please! I can't swim! Help!"

Malakai stood up and walked over to the pool. All that remained of the shark he had disemboweled were a few hunks of ragged meat. Bloody bits and pieces chummed the surface. The remaining sharks began circling Tanaka just as he spotted Malakai standing on the edge.

"Oh, thank God!" the Syndicate boss said, struggling to keep his head above water. "Malakai, please, help me. I can't swim. You want my daughter? You want money? Anything. It's yours. Just get me out of here."

Malakai didn't move. Just stared down at him. Thought about everything this man had done. The men he had ordered murdered. The carnage he had sanctioned. The beheading of Joe. The torture and abuse of his own daughter. Then he thought of Jesus' final words just a few minutes ago.

Even killers can show mercy sometimes.

Malakai locked eyes with Tanaka.

Sometimes, maybe. But not today.

He plucked a fragmentation grenade from his vest and pulled the pin. Voice as cold and grim as the angel of death, he rasped, "Catch this, asshole," and tossed the fragger on top of the thrashing crime lord.

"NOOOOOOOO—!!!!" Tanaka screamed.

His final word, cut off by the loud blast of the explosion. The grenade was right in front of his horrified face when it detonated. The point-blank burst of razored shrapnel scythed through his skull and shredded his brains, leaving a bloody mess strewn across the water.

The sharks moved in and tore the body apart, as they had done to so many victims before.

Malakai didn't wait around to watch the grisly feast. He helped Shiomi stand up, hopping on her remaining foot, arm around his neck for support and balance. She paused for just a moment to gaze into the pool where the sharks busily devoured her father's corpse. Malakai saw both satisfaction and sadness in her eyes. There was more of the latter than he ever would have expected.

"Come on," he said, "let's get you out of here."

"Where are we going?"

"Anywhere but here."

Together, arms around each other, they hobbled toward the door.

EPILOGUE
BARRA DE POTOSI, GUERRERO, MEXICO

8 MONTHS LATER...

MALAKAI WATCHED the sun sink into the horizon, painting the crystal blue water with dazzling rays of red and gold. There was peace inside him, something he hadn't felt for most of his life, and he was still learning to adjust.

Gentle waves rolled up onto the sand with a soothing, susurrating sound. Other regions in Mexico might be chock full of violent crime and clashing cartels and deep-rooted corruption, but this remote fishing village offered simple living and rustic, off-grid tranquility. For people trying to get away from the world, it was a great location.

He looked over at Shiomi, laying in a lounge chair beside him, sipping a glass of water as condensation ran down the side. Just beyond her he could see Asher and Larissa, similarly sprawled in their own loungers, air-drying after an evening swim. After his encounter with the sharks at Tanaka's mansion, Malakai preferred to keep his feet on dry land. Living *on* the ocean was one thing. Living *in* the ocean was another.

Needing a place to hide from the Syndicate following the execution of Tanaka, they had joined Asher and Larissa here in Barra de Potosi. The four of them had not planned on staying long—in the early days, they discussed relocating to Australia or Switzerland—but as they acclimated to the solitude and were accepted by the villagers, they realized this was as good a place as any to hunker down below the radar.

Down the beach, away from the actual village on the lagoon, they had built small bungalows. Some of the men in the village had helped them, demonstrating construction skills that matched their fishing abilities. Malakai and Asher had paid them well and the influx of money into the local economy no doubt went a long way to ensuring their acceptance within the community.

Barra de Potosi was also a place that valued its privacy and the villagers respected their wish for solitude. Maybe they recognized warriors in search of peace, scarred people looking for a place to heal, or maybe they didn't give it that much thought. Regardless, Malakai, Shiomi, Asher, and Larissa were treated well when they ventured into the village, but otherwise left alone. Live and let live seemed to be the motto, and given his new life, that was a creed Malakai could get behind.

He took a drink of his bottle of beer, some local brew that was better than expected. It wasn't a bottle of Red Dog from Joe's—man, he missed that guy—but it was crisp and cold and hit the spot as they all watched the sun drop ever lower into the sea.

Good friends, a beautiful woman, cold beer, peace and quiet, and a gorgeous sunset. There were worse ways to spend an evening.

Beside his chair was a small table and he set his bottle down on it, right next to the FNX-45 pistol. For all he knew, his old one was still rusting at the bottom of Tanaka's shark pool, but obtaining a replacement here in Mexico had proven fairly easy for someone accustomed to navigating the criminal underworld. With the cartels engaged in their brutal, never-ending war, black market weapon dealers were a dime a dozen in all the major cities. A couple of palms greased with cold, hard cash and bam, he was back in .45 caliber business.

On the other side of Shiomi and Larissa, Asher had his own little table with a Heckler & Koch HK45 Tactical semi-auto pistol lying next to a half-empty beer bottle. Malakai found it a little sad that even here in paradise, they both needed a weapon within easy reach, but that's just the way the dice rolled. They had enemies, and just because they had walked away to start new lives did not mean those enemies would stop hunting them. The bounties on their heads would not magically disappear.

His eyes focused on Shiomi again. The rays of the setting sun gleamed on her prosthetic leg, which was easy to see since she wore a bikini that contained less material than a handkerchief. Not that he was complaining. She admired the leg while Malakai admired everything else.

"You know," she said, "you hear a lot of negative things about the surgeons in Mexico, but I think he did a hell of a job on my leg."

"For what he charged us, he damn well better have."

"Worth every *peso*." She sipped her water. "But you know, I wonder if maybe I should get a good lawyer and sue the Syndicate for loss of limb. That was a good leg, easily worth a million or so." She turned her head and smiled at him. "What do you think? Want to call the Syndicate, let them know where we are, take them to court?"

"Waste of time," said Malakai. "You wouldn't have any chance of winning."

"Oh yeah? Why not?"

He grinned. "Because you haven't got a leg to stand on."

Her mouth fell open as she pretended to be shocked and insulted. "That is just so rude."

She leaned over and dumped her water in his lap.

"Hey!" he yelled. "Cut it out!"

Laughing, Shiomi climbed out of her lounge chair. "Relax, I'll go get you a towel."

"Good, because it looks like I pissed myself."

As she turned toward the bungalow, Shiomi suddenly stiffened. "There's somebody here."

Malakai and Asher were on their feet in a heartbeat, guns in hand, pointed at the intruder.

The middle-aged woman held up her hands, palms out to show she was unarmed. She had shoulder-length black hair streaked with gray and wore a dark business suit that must have been sweltering in this heat, yet she appeared cool, calm, and collected. She seemed unfazed by the pistols aimed at her.

"You won't be needing those," she said.

Malakai and Asher kept their .45s locked on target

and their fingers steady on the triggers. "We'll be the judge of that," Malakai replied.

"I'm here as a friend," the woman assured him, "not an enemy."

"We'll be the judge of that too."

"Given your circumstances, your mistrust is certainly understandable. After all, to those who are hunted, everyone and everything looks like a threat." Her eyes moved back and forth between the two men. "Do you know who I am?"

"I don't," Asher said. "But I'm guessing you're not the Avon lady."

The woman smiled thinly. "No, not exactly."

"I know who you are," Malakai said. "Senator Paula Olander."

The senator nodded. "That's right. May I lower my hands?"

"Suit yourself," said Malakai. "But I don't recommend any sudden moves."

"Where are your bodyguards?" Asher asked.

"They're close," Senator Olander replied, "but not too close. I thought it best if we have our conversation in private."

Malakai asked, "What conversation?"

"I believe you have some photographs of mine. I would like them back."

"I don't know what you're talking about."

"Don't be coy," said the senator. "It doesn't suit you."

"You don't know me, lady."

"Oh, for the last eight months or so, I've been learning all about you." She smiled, though it never quite reached her eyes. She might not be a full-fledged ice queen, but she was definitely frosty around the edges. "For example, are you aware that the Company has labeled you a rogue operative and issued a kill order?" She looked at Asher. "And your kill order is still active. You may have demolished the Black Talon program, but the Company still wants you dead. You're both considered shoot-on-sight status."

Malakai shrugged. "No surprise there."

"Yes, well, perhaps this might surprise you: the Company is currently training a new hunter-killer team and you two have been designated as their first targets."

Malakai rasped, "Tell them to bring it on."

"They came at me once and I'm still standing," said Asher. "Guess they want their asses kicked again."

"I suppose that is a possibility," Senator Olander admitted, "but why go through all that? I have a proposition for you. For both of you. If you agree, I'll have the kill orders lifted."

"You're full of crap," said Malakai. "That's not your call to make."

"I'm the head of the Senate Intelligence Committee."

"Doesn't mean you get to call the shots."

The senator sighed. "Don't be naïve, Malakai. You know how these things work. If I say the kill orders will be lifted, then they will be lifted. But not until we reach an understanding."

Malakai glanced over at Asher. His friend didn't look happy, but still gave him a slight nod. They both lowered their guns. "Let's hear your proposition," Malakai said.

"For starters—and this is nonnegotiable—you give me back my photos."

"Fine."

Olander looked surprised. "Really? Just like that? No argument?"

"I don't want your photos, Senator. They're not really my thing."

"I was young, stupid, and experimental," she explained, trying and failing to not sound defensive. "I'm sure there are parts of your youth that you're not proud of."

"Sure," Malakai replied. "But I didn't take pictures of them."

"Go ahead and judge me if it makes you feel better."

"I'm not judging you. Like you said, you were young and stupid."

"Did you make copies?" Olander asked.

"No."

"How do I know I can trust you?"

"You don't."

Senator Olander sighed. "We're going to have to learn how to trust each other if you agree to the next part of my proposition."

"And what would that be?"

Her gaze flicked back and forth between the two men. "I want you both to come work for me."

Asher spoke up. "Doing what?"

"What you do best."

"You mean killing."

"You're assassins. It's what you do."

"Speaking of that," Malakai said. "You know I killed your husband, right? I mean, yeah, sure, the Company ordered the hit, but I'm the one who pulled the trigger. Sure you still want me to work for you?"

"My husband was a rotten, lying, cheating son of a bitch and a traitor," the senator replied. "You did me—and this country—a favor by putting him down."

"Well, you're welcome, I guess," Malakai said. "But if you've done your homework like you claim, then you know we don't do that kind of work anymore. We walked away from that life. Now we just want to be left alone."

"You'll never be left alone," the senator countered. "The Company will never stop hunting you. Nor will the Syndicate, for that matter." She looked over at Asher. "And God only knows how long your truce with the Perelli organization will hold."

"And you can fix all that?" Malakai asked.

"I can't do much about the Syndicate or the Perellis," Olander replied. "But your biggest problem is the Company, and I can absolutely take care of that problem for you." She looked each man in the eye. "Face the facts, gentlemen, your best chance of survival is signing on with me."

"Tell us how the deal would work," Asher said.

Larissa, Shiomi, and Malakai all looked at him in surprise.

"Hold on a sec," Malakai said. "You're actually buying into this bullshit?"

"You're free to walk away," Asher replied. "I want to hear the mechanics."

"Why?"

"I have my reasons."

"Care to share them?"

"Not yet. Let her talk first."

"Fair enough. I guess talking never hurt anybody." Malakai gestured at Senator Olander. "Let's hear it."

"It's actually fairly simple," the senator said. "We want to bring Black Talon back into play."

"Wrong answer," Asher said. "Not interested."

Olander held up her hand. "Let me finish. We're not looking to *resurrect* Black Talon, we're looking to *revamp* it. Basically, you two would be Black Talon, an off-books team of assassins designed to be a lethal option to various threats."

"Sounds like the same thing we were doing before."

"It is and it isn't," the senator replied. "Yes, it's government wet work, but you wouldn't be working for the Company again. Only a handful of people aside from myself would even know about the new Black Talon."

"How about the president?" Malakai asked. "He one of them?"

She nodded. "Yes, he's in the loop, and he's sanctioned this project."

"What about support personnel?" Asher asked.

"There would be a support division, but for security purposes, it would be compartmentalized. You don't know who they are, they don't know you."

"That'll change. It always does."

The senator shrugged. "I'd be lying if I said that wasn't a possibility. The logistics of secrecy can be a real headache sometimes."

"How's this being funded?" Malakai asked.

"The usual slush funds."

"Same old black ops bullshit."

"How else would you expect it to be funded?" Olander said. "Some billionaire philanthropist living in a secret fortress hidden inside a volcano?"

Malakai ignored the sarcastic jab and turned his

head toward Asher. He was about to say something along the lines of, *Can you believe this crap?* but hesitated when he saw the pensiveness furrowing his friend's face.

Asher met his gaze for a moment, then turned to look at Larissa. Several heartbeats ticked by as he stared at the woman he loved with haunted eyes and Malakai sensed some internal struggle going on inside his friend.

Larissa couldn't see Asher, blinded eyes hidden behind mirrored sunglasses, but she seemed to sense that he was looking at her. Her lips twitched up in a little smile—a smile tinged with a touch of sadness—as she said, "I know what you're thinking, Gabe, and it's okay. Do what you think is right."

Asher nodded, turned back to Senator Olander, and said, "I'm in, but with one condition."

Malakai couldn't believe it. "You're going back to the life?"

"I have to."

"Why?"

Asher pointed at Larissa. "For her. As long as the Company dogs keep coming at us, she'll never be safe. If picking up my guns again is what it takes to get the kill order lifted, if that's what it takes to protect her, then that's what I have to do."

"Yeah, I get it." Malakai shook his head. "Ain't love a bitch sometimes?"

"So we have a deal?" the senator asked.

"Under one condition," Asher said. "Two, if you want to get technical."

"And they are?"

"I reserve the right to refuse targets and I reserve the right to go after targets I think have it coming."

Olander nodded. "I can live with that."

Shiomi stepped forward and touched Malakai's arm. "Malakai, you can't let him do this alone. He's your friend, your brother."

He looked at her, thinking of everything they had sacrificed to be together. "I told you I would lay down my guns, walk away from that life, and I meant it."

"And you did," she said, fingers squeezing reassuringly on his arm. "You kept your promise and I love you for that. But life doesn't always go the way we want, the way we hope. Sometimes things change and we have to change with them."

Malakai studied her face for a moment, then looked at Asher. "This really what you want to do?"

"I want to keep Larissa and Shiomi safe. I think this is the best option to accomplish that."

"You're ready to go back to living by the gun?"

Asher stared pointedly at the HK45 in his hand and the FNX-45 in Malakai's fist. "Let's face it, Malakai, we never *stopped* living by the gun."

Damn it, Malakai thought. *He's got a point.*

With a sigh, he trudged through the sand to his bungalow and returned with the black briefcase. As he handed the photos to Paula Olander, he said, "Let me make one thing perfectly clear, Senator. I expect those kill orders lifted as soon as you get cell service. If anyone comes for us, we will unleash holy hell on them. Scorched earth, burn it to the ground, no survivors. And when we're done with them, you'll be next. Are we straight on that?"

The senator accepted the briefcase with a look of relief on her face and nodded curtly. "No need for threats. I am a woman of my word. Obviously I can't control what the Syndicate does, or what the Perelli family does, but no one from the Company will bother you again." She smiled thinly. "Besides, you two are back on the team. I'll be in touch."

With that, she walked away.

Shiomi slipped an arm around Malakai's waist and leaned into him as Asher asked, "Do you believe her?"

As the sun sank lower into the horizon, Malakai said, "Actually, yeah, I do. I think she's shooting straight with us."

"I know it's not what you wanted," Asher said. "Hell, it's not what I wanted either. But I think it was the right call."

"It was," Malakai agreed. He put his arm around Shiomi's shoulders and pulled her close, a beautiful treasure that he never wanted to let go. "I don't care what I have to do, as long as I've got her."

Asher smiled and looked at Larissa, her red hair on fire from the setting sun. "I know how you feel."

Arms around each other, Malakai and Shiomi turned and walked down the beach. Malakai knew there was no way to completely crush the Syndicate, so they would forever live with those crosshairs on their backs. And now that he and Asher were going back into the guns-for-hire game, there would be more crosshairs to come.

But he had Shiomi by his side and Asher at his back.

That was good enough for him.

WATCH FOR: THE ASSASSIN'S RESURRECTION
BY MARK ALLEN

WHEN THE PAST WON'T STAY DEAD, ONLY BLOOD AND BULLETS CAN SETTLE THE SCORE.

In the explosive return of the *Assassin's* series, the covert black ops program Black Talon has been resurrected—and this time, Asher and Malakai are the tip of the spear in a brutal campaign to take down a human trafficking pipeline. But what begins as a precision strike quickly detonates into a full-blown war when a New York mob boss partners with ruthless Russian gangsters, triggering a war no one saw coming.

When an innocent girl is abducted in a retaliatory strike, the mission turns personal. Asher's haunted by the sins of his past —he killed her father. Saving the girl may be the closest thing to redemption he'll ever get.

Adding fuel to the fire, an attack on Asher's house results in a confrontation with an old enemy that tears open emotional scars. Meanwhile, Malakai is marked for death by a shadow Syndicate assassin, and a traitor inside Black Talon is feeding their enemies every move.

With time running out, bullets flying, and loyalties fractured, Asher and Malakai must fight through a war zone of betrayal, blood, and brotherhood. The only way out...is one bullet at a time.

Can two battle-scarred killers defy the ghosts of their past to save an innocent life—or will this mission end in annihilation?

AVAILABLE AUGUST 2025

ABOUT THE AUTHOR

Mark Allen was raised by an ancient clan of ruthless ninjas—though breaking his oath of silence to say so might get him killed. When not practicing shuriken throws or hunting flea markets for a katana, Mark writes high-octane action fiction. He calls it "guns 'n' guts"—packed with twin Micro-Uzis, headshots galore, and punchy prose.

He wrote his first story at 16, won a regional contest soon after, and later published *The Assassin's Prayer*, which sold over 10,000 copies in its first year. Originally optioned by Showtime, the novel blends raw emotion with brutal action, earning Mark a loyal readership.

He lives in the Adirondacks with a skeptical wife, two martial arts–averse daughters, and enough firepower to keep door-to-door salesmen at bay.